Hopeful Monsters

Hiromi Goto

Hope*ful*

MONSTERS

«stories»

ARSENAL
PULP PRESS
Vancouver

Second printing: 2010

ARSENAL PULP PRESS
101, 211 East Georgia Street
Vancouver, BC
Canada V6A 1Z6
arsenalpulp.com

The publisher gratefully acknowledges the support of the Canada Council for the Arts and the British Columbia Arts Council for its publishing program, and the Government of Canada through the Canada Book Fund and the Government of British Columbia through the Book Publishing Tax Credit Program for its publishing activities.

Design by Solo

Printed and bound in Canada

National Library of Canada Cataloguing in Publication

Goto, Hiromi, 1966–
    Hopeful monsters : stories / Hiromi Goto.
ISBN 1-55152-157-1
    I. Title.
PS8563.O8383H66 2004   C813'.54   C2004-900678-9

For Tiger Goto,
who shows me, through example,
how to walk lightly into the darkness,
whistling as you go. . . .
I respect *and* love you.

Night

When your sight tilts like that
You laugh out loud in your sleep, you know. Did you know? You laugh out loud in your sleep. There are heads of hakusai in the basement starting to dry out before they have a chance to rot because of the heat from the dryer in what would otherwise be a very cold basement. It would be a terrible waste to throw them out because they are not so bad that I couldn't peel away the topper leaves and use the rest but I can't bear to touch them because they're garden hakusai, grown outside, and there are bugs gone cocooned or chrysalis or whatever in the crinkle leaves and it'll make me scream if any touched my hands. (Three women sit around a Formica table in the kitchen.)

Cup
I like to sleep with the window open but you prefer it closed and I have to stick my feet outside the covers if I want to get any sleep at all, but the one drawback to sleeping with the window open is that the magpies squawk at sunrise and I have to get out of bed and slam my palm against the glass until they fly away while you go to the fridge for a cup of cold mugi-cha but forget to bring me any and the baby wakes up from all the noise. (Three women at 1:37 AM.)

9

Two Linger
Sometimes you say a word out loud and it's just that there is only the one falling from your mouth like a small bone or a stone from a plum and there's nothing to hold it up against so I have to prod you with sticks of questions but you never say anything else and only nuzzle below my breasts with your fingertips in your sleep. (The grandmother sips, noisily, her beer and sucks the residue from her teeth in smacks.)

Tick   Tock

It's loud, you know. At night.

SometimesIhateyousomuchIcan'tevenbeartoliebesideyouandI'dwish you'dgoandsleeponthecouchbutyouneverdosoIhavetoleaveifIwant youtogo.

It's loud, you know. At night.

Tick

                    Tock

Three women sit around a Formica table in the kitchen. Three women at 1:37 AM. The grandmother sips, noisily, her beer and sucks the residue from her teeth in smacks. The mother turns to her daughter.

"You should go to sleep soon. The baby's going to wake up at least once."

"Yeah, soon," the daughter says, wanting to sit a while longer, in the quiet, with the women.

"Of course, if your father has another dream like the other night, everybody'll be up," the mother laughs.

"What happened?"

"Such a colossal racket! I thought my heart would burst!" says the grandmother. Slurping the last drops of beer from her cup.

"Your father started screaming at the top of his voice in the middle of the night. Thrashing about on his bed. I was sleeping downstairs, but I woke up, it was so loud. I ran upstairs. Grandmother ran in from her room too."

"I thought he was dying," the grandmother says.

"He was awake by then and such sweating and panting! I asked him what he dreamt about. And he said, his voice all quivering, 'Two women were trying to crawl into bed beside me while I was sleeping. Two strange women!'"

The mother glances at the grandmother and they burst into laughter, snapping the humming night stillness.

"I said to him, 'Well, what are you so frightened about? Most people would love to have two strange women join them in bed!' But he only shook his head, got a drink of water, and went back to his room." They laugh again and the daughter laughs with them.

"The poor man," the daughter says. "We shouldn't make fun." She rises from her chair and goes to the fridge for a beer. She twists it open, pours some into her grandmother's cup, then takes a long swallow from the bottle.

"I think I'll join you," her mother says and pours herself some rye and Diet Coke.

The women sit together, drinking.

"I had the most frightening nightmare last night," the mother says.

"What was it?" asks the daughter, picking at the label of her beer with a fingernail.

"I dreamt I was sleeping in the spare bedroom, so I didn't realize I was dreaming because I was dreaming I was sleeping, which I was. Anyways! There I was, sleeping, and something wakes me up. A rustle, rustle, then tapping. Kon, kon, kon. Like a hammer or something. Kon, kon, kon. And I lay there for quite some time, just listening, until I realize that it's an awfully strange time of night to be doing any construction work. So I slowly open my eyes and there beside my bed, in the wall, there's a great jagged hole – like someone has been using a pick-axe on it. Inside the room it's night dark, but outside, framed by the jagged edge of the broken wall, it's a grey dawn colour. I thought to myself, 'That's strange,' and then a German Shepherd sticks his head inside the hole to look at me! But I like dogs, so I'm not frightened. I just think, 'Why, there's a dog looking at me.' The dog pulls his head out and leaves and I can see a pair of legs standing right outside the hole."

"The dog's?" asks the grandmother.

"No, a man's! I can only see from his mid-thigh down to his feet, just outside my room, and a long wooden handle stands vertically beside his legs and I know it's the pick-axe! My heart's pounding in my ears, but I can't move, can't move, can only watch as he bends down, looks through the hole, and sees me watching. He crams his head inside, shoving his shoulders, trying to force his knee through and I yell! I yelled, 'Dorobo! Dorobo! Dorobo!' until I woke myself up."

"Well, I didn't hear a thing," says the grandmother, peering at her daughter. "And there's nothing much in this house a thief would want to steal," she adds. Sips from her cup.

"What do you dream of, Grandmother?"

"Oh I have frightening dreams, girl. Something terrible!" She says nothing more, and her daughter and granddaughter sit, watching her, waiting for her to continue. Outside, a late cricket begins to chirp and the cat wanders in from the living room, jumps lightly onto the mother's lap. The mother snuggles the cat between her breasts, cat rubbing his head against her chin.

"A very strange thing, this. Every time, it's a new dream. Every moment, it's brand new, and I don't realize I've dreamt it a hundred, a thousand times before until after I wake up." The grandmother gazes beyond her fingers clutching the cup. Strokes the plastic cup with pebbled fingertips, her other hand a knuckle around the handle. The cat watches her stroking fingers with half-closed eyes, his pupils full and black. The mother stares at the top of the cat's head and glides her hand down his gleaming back. Her daughter watches the grandmother's face. The sharp bone of cheek, the hollows around her eyes, her throat.

"I don't know why, but I have all my clothes on, you know. Everyone else is naked. And I think, 'How strange,' but not because everyone is naked. Something else bothers me, only I don't, I can't see it." She leans into her cup and takes a sip of beer. Smack. Smack. The young woman leans back in her chair and sets her feet on the seat opposite, between her mother's legs, still intently watching her grandmother's face.

"Everyone starts kissing and touching each other. Men and

women, women and women, men and men. And it's good. Healthy. Then a woman I've never met before comes to me and starts touching my breasts and stroking my neck and I feel fine. Yes, fine. Then a man, a stranger, he pushes her away and starts to kiss me. I'm not sure about this, but he keeps on kissing me and kneels down to kiss my breasts through my clothes. I'm still half-pleasured from the woman touching me, but it's going away and my head is clearing. There's something wrong. I know it now so close. Very, very wrong. I feel his erection against my thigh and he grabs me close, close, no! Something hard stabs beneath my chin, pushing up and up against the bottom of my chin and I shove him back and back and I see him. I really see him. Oh god. . . . He is deformed. He is deformed. He has two erections. One between his legs and oh god, one at the base of his throat. A penis rising at an angle from the hollow of his collarbones and mat-mat of hair and his scrotum sags upon his chest. And I feel sick. I feel sick and turn and look and all the men. I can see. They are deformed. Every one of them."

The three women sit silently. Only the sound of the cat.

"It's funny," the grandmother says, "how frightening the dreams are when you are in them, but if you try to explain them, they never sound that way." She sucks the last bit of beer from her cup and turns to her granddaughter. "And what about you, child. What do you dream?"

The young woman rolls bits of the beer label into tiny pills. She looks up and sees her mother and grandmother watching her face. "I don't dream," she says. They remain silent.

"At least," she adds, "none that I can remember."

14

From upstairs, there is a sleepy wail and the three women are still. Perhaps the baby will go back to sleep. Perhaps. . . . But the cry gathers momentum, no longer sleepy, rising in pitch to become anger. The young woman finishes her beer in three long swallows and burps. She picks up a baby bottle from the draining board and fills it with warm water from the tap, screws the nipple on.

"Well, see you in the morning," she says, and thumps softly upstairs.

The grandmother and mother sit at the kitchen table. They didn't notice the cricket had stopped chirping until it begins again.

Upstairs, it is quiet.

Osmosis

The texture of night.

Everyone is asleep after drinking too many rye and Cokes, too many bottles of beer, and you are tired-aching in your joints from the alcohol lingering there. Wood smoke. Stub your toe on a cooler, should have worn thongs, never knew there was cactus in Alberta until today. The humped backs of canoes flipped upside down on the shore. It is still hot even though the moon has set. Peel sticky undershirt off like a sausage casing and thumb shorts, panties down thighs. Your arms limp beside you, curl toes into crumbly sand. Hesitate. Lift cracked heel, arch, the fleshy pad of foot, slowly, like an ancient bird. Slip one cautious foot into liquid smooth. One foot on land. The clasp of water cool, like a bracelet around your ankle and shivers run up your leg, spread across your back. No wind. No wind. Just the lap of water. Just the muted roar of blood coursing and your body fills with the night. You think you are alone.

You stepped up to the rim of the water and when you placed one foot inside, the silent circles of your movement lapped against my neck. I flicked back my head because I thought it was some man drunk with intent, but I saw a soft shaped shadow and a gleaming ankle. You cannot see me, the moon long set and short black hair sleekwet against my head. I am still, watching your stillness.

You look up.

Ankle softly clasped in the water and the sky swirls above you. The stars are too close so you shut your eyes to their clamour and lean thoughts toward the water. You want to think only of the water but there is the chirp of crickets and the distant snores of drunken friends. A splash in the outer limits of sight, but you think it is a fish or a bird. Perhaps a pebble, dropping from a steep embankment. How your laughing father threw you out into the ocean, the first time you ever saw a large body of water. Sank slowly, eyes open, burning, the seaweed looked like eels and your hiccupped lungs full of liquid salt. When your sister fished you out, you couldn't believe how painful it was to vomit sea water through your nose, the back of your throat stinging of salt for days. You know you shouldn't remember this. You were only two. Never ever learned how to swim, but you like the texture. Wish that you could trust it.

I want you to step inside the water and lean against its back. If you took one more step you would see the shape of my head darker than the water. The mud between my toes is cool and slides slick between revulsion and pleasure. A tiny mouth nibbles the skin on my calf and I almost giggle. Kappa, I think. Kappa. Not a drowner of children or an anus-sucking monster. But a tiny green froggish thing with a tickly mouth. Kappa, I think, and I almost say the word aloud.

Close your eyes.

The after-image of stars. Wanting to move, trying to move the other foot into the water. You rest most of your weight on the foot on land and it has been still too long, takes movement upon itself. You know the flesh of your thigh, belly, are jiggling, but the black of night and the heat of quiet is enough to dim the movement. The clasp of water around your ankle makes you feel beautiful. You are beautiful. You know you will not be beautiful when the sun rises tomorrow. Both feet will be on solid ground and you'll have to force your heavy body to mince around cacti you never knew grew in Alberta until yesterday. People will fight about who gets to cook and who will end up washing waxy bacon grease off cast iron frying pans. Watch, with envy and disgust, people crawling out of tents that are not their own. Someone will step on a cactus and you'll mince even more carefully. You will not be beautiful tomorrow.

Shiver the water cooling, evaporating from the surface, and I have been still too long. The cold seeps into chest, the hollow of my lungs. Breathing deep. Longing. Wrinkled hands to my breasts floating weightless and such a strange sensation. My hair starts to dry, stirs against my forehead.

Open your eyes.

But the night is still dark when you imagined that it might be lighter. Realize the lightness you felt was the cool breeze tracing the curve of spine. Skin pimpling from your wrists, up your arms to your neck. It feels so good you almost pee, standing where you are. One foot in, one foot out. You wish you could trust the water enough to take another step. Maybe two. You want to stand at least waist deep so you can pee inside the water. You know the hot urine from your body will seep into the fluid all around you and in that moment, all would be one. You would be able to lie back, sink smoothly without a ripple, and assume the texture of water. Osmosis. You will not drown. You are water. And when you rise, you will take a part of that with you. When you wake the next morning people will come up to you and say you look different. That you look really nice. You will smile, not saying a thing, and two girls and a guy will ask you out on a date for next Friday.

The stars are tilting away from me and the breeze has picked up to a wind. My toes begin to ache in mud, my lower lip starts to quiver. I could call out. I could call out. But I don't even know your name. You don't know I'm here. And I may have imagined you as I have imagined myself.

I slide backward, underwater, slicing down through dark fluid soft as egg yolk. Slowly twist my body around. Kick the mud with my feet and propel upward. My head breaks the surface and I start swimming to the other side of the lake. I imagine I hear a voice softly murmur, "Kappa."

Tilting

Obā-chan was the first to come out of the terminal gates, pushed in her wheelchair by a bearded Canadian Airlines man in a navy blue sweater. Her bamboo walking stick pointed straight up and down like an exclamation mark. The navy blue sweater man all brisk brisk and a quick fake smile hidden by his facial hair.

"Obā-chan," I said, "you don't look too tired." And tried to hug her as best I could around her walking stick, the cool metal arms of the wheelchair. Kunio held Kenji up, dangling the child in front of Obā-chan so that she could give him a kiss, but he squirmed away from her face.

"He just got up from his nap, so he's a little grumpy," I said, excusing him. Obā-chan smiled wanly. Kunio juggled Kenji on to his left arm and bent down to give Obā-chan a quick peck.

"I'll just take her down to the luggage area," the navy blue sweater man said, and swung Obā-chan around us, pushed her brusquely down the hall. Kunio and I watched him stride stride, his back straight and the exclamation of Obā-chan's bamboo walking stick. Swallowed by the elevator.

Dad finally left the helicopter game he had spent six dollars of quarters on and approached us. "Where's your mom?"

"She hasn't come out yet," I said.

"Do you have any more quarters?"

Kunio jostled Kenji from his left arm to his right and stuck his hand in his jean pocket. Made a fist and pulled it out. He opened his fingers and revealed a dirty piece of unchewed gum, a toothpick, six pennies, a dime, and three quarters. Dad picked out the quarters from Kunio's palm, said, "Thanks," and went back to the game. We watched him lift his leg to straddle the seat of the helicopter. Slip two quarters into the slot and grip the control stick. He jerked and pushed the controls, his body weaving, jolting with the movement of the machine. Computerized sounds of missiles being launched and bombs dropped. Sharp fingers jabbed my shoulder and I jumped around. Mom's face all red and puffy and standing so close that her panting breath stirred my bangs.

"Your face is swollen. You look tired," I managed.

"I'm exhausted! My head is spinning!"

"Something smells like takuwan," I said, sniffing the air. "Your hand luggage smells like takuwan."

"Don't tell me about it! The takuwan opened up in my hand luggage somewhere over Japan and it's been like that the whole flight home. All the way from Tokyo to Korea to Vancouver to Calgary, the thing was smelling up the inside of the plane and not a thing I could do. Your father's sister gave it to me."

"Oh, no," I said, stepping away from her.

Kunio leaned over. "Welcome home," he said and gave Mom a peck on the cheek. Mom beamed, then turned to Kenji. "Give me a kiss."

Kenji leaned and gave her an open-mouthed slobber and she wiped it off with her fingers, looking pleased.

"Where's your father?" Mom asked.

"On that helicopter," I pointed. We all turned and watched him jerking around on the seat of the game, dropping bombs and firing missiles in complete absorption. Kenji squirmed and wriggled.

"Aiyai! Aiyai! Aaaiiyaaiiiii!" he hollered. Kunio let him down and he ran, laughing, towards the escalators. Kunio loped after him.

"The smell was just awful. And that was that. There wasn't a thing I could do and now everyone will go away thinking, 'It's true. Oriental people. They smell funny,'" Mom said.

"You shouldn't say Oriental, Mom. You should say Asian."

"Asian, Oriental, it doesn't change the way takuwan smells," she said. "Where's your grandmother?"

"The Canadian Airlines man in the navy blue sweater took her down to the luggage area."

"That man!" Mom said. "I don't know what his rush rush is all about. I've been chasing him ever since I got off that plane and me with all this hand luggage to carry."

"Here," I held out my hand, "let me take that for you.

"God!" I exclaimed. "It weighs a ton! What do you have in there?"

"I told you! Oh, my head is spinning." Mom closed her eyes.

"Kunio!" I yelled. He was at the other end of the terminal, in front of the toy shop with Kenji on his shoulders, watching a teddy bear on a tightrope glide back and forth on a unicycle. "Kunio, come help with the luggage!"

"Hiroshi!" Mom yelled, "Hiroshi, get off that helicopter and help!" Dad jostled the control stick a few more times, dropped a few more bombs, then flung both hands into the air. Dad and Kunio reached us at the same time.

"I think that Kenji might have pooped," Dad said.

"It's not Kenji," I explained. "Some takuwan exploded in Mom's hand luggage."

"Oh," Dad said. He turned to Kenji. "Sorry."

Kunio picked up two of Mom's bags and Dad took the other. I held Kenji's hand and we walked towards the escalator, Mom panting behind us muttering softly, "My head is spinning. The ground is heaving beneath my feet." I lifted Kenji's hands above his head when we reached the bottom of the escalator so he wouldn't stumble, then let him go. Laughing, he ran toward the luggage conveyor belt. The navy blue sweater was still standing behind Obā-chan's chair, making a smile face behind his beard. He helped her out of the chair and sat her on the plastic covered bench amidst piles of luggage and travel-tired people. Obā-chan nodded her thanks to him and he lipped a smile again and strode strode away.

"I wonder if we should have given him a tip," Mom said.

"It's not like he's a bellhop," I sighed. "It's not like Obā-chan is luggage."

"I know!" Mom said. "I'm just saying that it might have been a nice gesture."

"Why don't you sit down?" I asked.

"I will," she said. "I'll sit down right now and never get up again."

"Where's Kenji?" Dad asked.

We looked up, sweeping a quick circumference, and spotted him at the other end of the terminal, pushing a luggage cart as fast as he could, people dodging around him and angrily looking for parents to attach him to.

"I'll get him," Kunio said, and jogged after him. There was a general surge toward the luggage belt and bags started spewing from the chute.

"Oh," Mom said, "here it comes." And stood right in front so she would be in the best position to grab. Dad rocked back and forth on his heels, his arms crossed. I sat down beside Obā-chan on the bench. Took her hand in mine.

"How was your trip?" I asked. "How was Masao-ojichan?"

"The hospital was very small. Six beds in each room. There was one window but it faced the north so little sunlight came in. The only sounds to be heard were of old people in discomfort. The nurses were very young and it made one feel that much older, that much weaker. The ward had patients with head problems, so sometimes people would wander in and talk to you like they were old acquaintances continuing a conversation already started. Then a young girl in a white uniform would rush in and bow and apologize and lead them away. Masao-chan was all curled in upon himself when we first went to see him, and I thought he looked like a peanut and I was afraid to touch him because he was so brittle. 'Masao-chan,' I said, 'Masao-chan, we've come.' And he opened his eyes and looked up at me and I don't know what he saw but it must have been nice because he smiled and went back to sleep. We sat in the room with those sick men, your mom and I, and we rubbed his legs and arms with a warm cloth and wiped his face and wriggled his toes and fingers and washed his hair. The nurse brought us some hot ocha and we sipped loudly so it would sound like home, and we ate early green-skinned oranges. He didn't wake up, so we went to your mom's cousin's house. They made us a great feast, but we were too tired to eat so we talked and took a bath and went to sleep. We ate the leftover food in the morning and took the bus to the hospital again and when we went into Masao-chan's room, he was already awake and so surprised to see us. 'Onē-san!' he said, 'Onē-san!' And he couldn't say anything else because he was crying and we were crying too."

Kenji's wails echoed in the high ceiling. I looked up. He was sitting on the floor holding his knees, and Kunio crouched beside him, talking softly.

"'You're here,' he said, 'you came.' 'Yes,' I said, 'we were here yesterday but you were tired and you didn't see us.' 'I saw you,' he said, 'I just didn't know it was you.' I tucked the blankets more warmly around his body and he reached up to touch my hand and hold it. He was so cold! 'You're like ice,' I said, and rubbed, rubbed his hands between mine. He smiled at your mom. 'And you too, Miya-chan, and you too.' Your mom leaned over his bed and hugged him Canada-style and he was quite surprised but pleased, you could tell. Then she took his icy feet and rubbed and rubbed them until they were poka poka like baked sweet potatoes. 'Have you seen my wife yet?' he asked. 'Kimiko is not well. She was taking care of me too much and she weakened her own body. Her back is no good. She can't move very well.' 'We haven't seen her yet,' I said. 'We talked to her on the phone and she's coming to your daughter's house this afternoon. Ten years is too long since I saw you both.'"

"Hiroshi!" Mom called, "Hiroshi, help me with this luggage." Dad ambled to where she was sliding a suitcase from the conveyor belt. Plunking it on the ground beside her, she imperiously pointed to a large cardboard box. Dad lifted it with his back rather than his knees. Winced. Mom stared up the chute, willing her last bags to come out more quickly.

"Kimiko-chan had aged. There is nothing else you could say. Ten years is a lot if you are seventy to begin with, and my brother's illness had made her stoop well into ninety. 'We thought he was going to die,' she said, her voice wobbling. She held both of my hands. 'I was getting ready for his funeral.' 'Don't say that,' I said, 'it's not so.' 'Yes,' she said, 'but it is better now that you and Miya-chan are both here. It is better.' And she sat down on a chair and smiled her special smile. And it felt good, to be there with my brother and his wife and Miya-chan, no matter what the reason for being there was. We were together. That was what was most important at that moment."

I wasn't looking at Obā-chan, just watching people pass in front of me while her words flowed over my body. From the side of my face I could feel her nodding now and then as she stroked one hand over the other. The sound of Kenji's laughter.

26

"I couldn't stay with Masao-chan every day at the hospital. It would be too much for me. So your mom's cousin took me to Masao and Kimiko-chan's. Kimiko-chan and I, two old women drinking green tea and eating yō-kan and trying to keep each other healthy as best we could. We talked about a lot of old things as old people will, but we talked of new things too. And Miya-chan, she went to the hospital every day from her cousin's house because it was closer. She went every day and changed his sheets and washed his body and made him tea and talked and talked and massaged his skinny legs and arms and washed his face, his hair. She didn't go to meet her friends for coffee or drinks and she didn't go shopping or sightseeing. She stayed with Masao-ojichan and took care of his body. And he got stronger. He got stronger and he could sit up and eat some porridge. He started walking to the washroom and asking for books to read."

Kenji squirmed his way between my knees, his head tipped back, looking up at my face. He reached down and tugged at the crotch of his pants.

"I have to change Kenji's diaper," I said, my hand on Obā-chan's shoulder. I picked up my oversize purse and clasped Kenji's hand. As we walked toward the washroom I could still hear Obā-chan's voice behind me.

"It was a shame. I hadn't seen Masao-chan for ten years and when I finally went, I couldn't even visit with him. Five times only I saw him even though we were there for three weeks. I had much to tell him, but my body too weak to sit at a hospital all day. All I could do was know that he was a lot closer to me than before. Talking to Kimiko-chan and where did all the time go? Three weeks pass like water if you are wishing it otherwise. And I thought about staying. I did. But what would I do? An old woman with two other old people and Miya-chan couldn't stay. No, Miya-chan a grandmother already, so hard to believe, and her home is not there any longer. No, I could not stay and my daughter, I saw how her face changed when we landed in Calgary. The edges around her eyes disappeared, this her home now. And I am home with her. Masao-chan convalescing, and Kimiko-chan's back is a little better. I can rest easy for a while and enjoy my great grandson. And when he talks, when he can talk to me, I will listen."

When we got back, Kunio was eating a soft ice-cream cone and Dad was sitting on the bench next to Obā-chan. Mom, at the next bench over, dug through her luggage, looking at this and that. Kenji ran to Kunio and raised both arms. "Up-poo! Up-poo!" Kunio lifted him onto his lap and they took turns licking the ice-cream.

I stood next to Mom as she dug through her luggage. "What are you doing?" I asked.

"I'm looking for your gifts."

"Why don't you do that when you get home? There's no need to do it now. Look, we just came because we're glad that you're home safely."

"I want to give you the presents now," she said, looking in this bag, then that one, removing a box, a couple of boxes, a small sack.

"These are for Kenji!" she said happily, holding up two pairs of shoes.

"Oh, that's great!" I said. "His feet are growing so quickly, I can't afford to keep up with them."

"That's what I thought," she beamed, and held the shoes beside Kenji's feet. They were at least three sizes too big.

"That's all right," Kunio said, "he can wear them when he's older."

Mom went back to her parcels and handed Kunio a large carton of expensive sake and a box of specialty rāmen noodles. He glowed with pleasure. "Thank you," he said. "Thank you very much. These must have been heavy."

Mom returned to her bags with a satisfied grin. She passed me a box of hot Korean salted pollock roe. My mouth watered.

Dad got in on it. "Here's some pickles. Take some pickles."

"Not the one that exploded, please," I said, flapping my hand.

Mom still searched for more. "I know I'm forgetting something," she muttered, rummaging through messy clothing.

"It can wait," Dad said, and she finally stopped. She lifted both her hands to her face and smacked her cheeks.

"I gained a lot of weight, didn't I?"

"Oh, I thought your face was just swollen from retaining water and being tired after the long flight." I stared at her chin, wondering if it hung a little lower than before.

"It was the fish," Mom closed her eyes dreamily. "The fish was so incredibly good."

"Most people eat fish to lose weight, Mom."

"I think it's great that you ate so much you gained weight," Kunio said.

"It was fish to die for. At least gain fifteen pounds for, anyway."

"Should we go for supper somewhere? I'm feeling a bit hungry," Dad said.

"*Dad*," I said, "I don't think Obā-chan is up to sitting through a meal. She probably wants to go home."

"Yes, I'd like to go home and get some rest," Obā-chan nodded.

"Okay," Dad said, raising both hands, palms outward. "I was just thinking about supper, that's all. I thought everyone might be hungry."

"We can eat some of the rāmen I brought home," Mom said. "Well, I know I'm forgetting something, but it'll have to wait."

"Thank you for all the gifts," Kunio bobbed his head. "It must have been very heavy for you."

"Not at all. After all that you've done for us," Mom beamed.

"We didn't do very much at all," I said. "We're just glad that you're home and everything."

"Well, let's go!" Mom said.

"I'll bring the car around," Dad said. Ambled toward the exit.

Kenji started his, "Uhhhhn, uhhhhn, uhhhhhhhhn!" and I looked down. His face and hands were covered in ice-cream.

"Oh, for goodness sake," Mom said and dug in her coat pocket for a Kleenex. She wrapped it around her forefinger and spat on it and wiped Kenji's face. Kenji squirmed. Kunio started loading Mom's bags on to luggage carts. When Dad returned, he and Kunio pushed the carts out, Mom following with Kenji in tow. Obā-chan leaned on my arm and her bamboo walking stick. Dad had brought a pillow and two sleeping bags for Obā-chan so she could lie down on the way home. Mom settled her in the back seat and then got in the front.

"Thank you for coming," she said.

"We'll come and visit when you're rested up." I patted Obā-chan's shoulder, then shut the door.

"Bye," said Kunio.

Dad saluted and got into the car. As he pulled away from the curb, Kenji, belatedly, started shouting.

"Bye, bye, bye, bye, bye!"

Obā-chan was lying down so I couldn't see her, but her hand was raised above the seat and she was waving.

Driving, the roads icy and dust-dry wind. Kenji in the back, looking for buses and big trucks. The inside of the car warm. I didn't want to do anything, but feeling this gap, this longing, a sense of something unsaid and wanting to fill it. Something tinged the edges of memory and tilting.

"You know, when we arrived in Narita, I had this strange feeling that my feet weren't quite solid on the ground. The edges of my hemisphere felt skewed the tiniest bit and the ground leaned back against my sole with every step I took. It was a neat sort of feeling if you're not prone to motion sickness. And I was thinking that maybe the ground was trying to tell me something. That I couldn't just land and feel right at home. That there was a period of transition or something to go through."

"Maybe you were just jet-lagged," Kunio suggested.

"No, I don't think so, because the feeling was there for the whole trip and I was over being jet-lagged by the third day. No, it was something to do with the land and my walking on it and what that meant and all sorts of things. I don't know. You know what I mean?"

"No, not really."

"The whole time I was there I had this feeling I wasn't ever quite there. Like I was in a box made of Saran Wrap and I could see out in a thinly distorted sort of way, and people could see me too, but always through a barrier. Sometimes I felt lonely and other times I felt almost nothing at all, and I really can't remember the details of the trip except for the love hotel and the earthquake."

"That earthquake was one of the biggest ones I've felt."

"It was funny because the earthquake happened after that snow blizzard in Tokyo and everyone kept saying we must have brought the snow with us from Canada because it almost never snows in Tokyo and never so much at once. Remember, we walked from the subway station and the blizzard blasting on our faces and the snow sticking because it was so wet and Kenji on your back hiding his face and almost falling asleep because he was so tired. We stopped at the store to buy beer and snacks and instant rāmen and onigiris and Hide buying a giant chocolate bar and we all laughed. And you slipped going up the stairs to Takeshi's apartment and cut your hand and blood on the snow so brilliant, so beautiful. Nobu arriving late, after we'd drank a lot of beer, Kenji sleeping in the next room and us eating instant rāmen out of the Styrofoam containers. Remember? We took pictures and drank some more and ate the snacks and I was the first one to go sleep. And I don't remember when you came to bed, but something woke me up. Something familiar, but its relationship to place was so skewed, I woke up with a jolt and sat upright. The room was moving beneath us and the weird sense of something I'd always felt as motionless heaving like nausea. And things toppled off the TV and the bookshelves and cupboards and I leaned over Kenji who slept through the whole thing, me leaning over him and making a tent with my arms and you sat up in your blankets and said, 'Big one,' and I absolutely couldn't believe your factual tone of voice. Not leaning over to protect me or Kenji, just calmly sitting up in your futon. And I could hear Hide in the next room, sleeping on the floor with Takeshi and Nobu, could hear him through the paper-thin walls. 'Big. Big,' he said, in the exact same tone of voice as yours and I couldn't believe it and I started laughing."

"You sure can remember a lot of details for someone who hardly remembers the trip."

"I remember the things I remember really clearly. And that love hotel."

"Well, I don't know why you remember the love hotel. It wasn't very memorable for me. Nothing happened."

"That's why it was so memorable. *Because* nothing happened. I had all this anticipation of a love hotel experience after watching those Japanese dramas and cheap movies and hearing about them and wanting to experience this really sleazy thing. Only that wasn't the way it turned out at all. I mean, I was amazed at how the whole thing was set up. Nothing could be more clinical about illicit sex.

Kenji at your mom's and us driving back to your parents' place after visiting your friend and all over I saw the love hotels' lights flicker-flacker like Christmas at home, only here it was for sex and I said, 'Let's go to a love hotel.' And you said, 'Do you really want to?' and I said, 'Yeah, it would be neat and I want to see what it's like inside.' So you pulled into the next one, and I was a little disappointed because it didn't have a theme. It didn't have a castle front and wasn't shaped like a spaceship like others I'd seen, but we were pressed for time so I didn't say anything and you pulled into the underground parking and into an empty stall, not that there were many left, and you showed me how you pulled the gate behind your car so people couldn't see your license plate or recognize your vehicle. I was amazed at the thought put into the arrangement. And we went into the lobby but there wasn't a desk, or manager, or people, nothing. Only this great lighted panel on the wall with photographs of each room so you could pick the one of your choice, like a giant pop machine, only the ones that weren't lit up were occupied, and there were only three rooms left to choose from so I picked the one I liked the best and pressed the button and the keys came out of the slot. I was so pleased that I laughed. We took the elevator to our floor, six, and we got to our room without passing a single soul. No sounds, no moans, no nothing. It's like we're the only people in this place in a city of millions. We went into our room, but no sleaze there, either. It looked like a nice hotel room with an extra big bathroom and bathrobes on the bed and everything. So we decided we should get our money's worth and took a bath and washed each other and me feeling not exactly erotic or sleazy and you not either and we decided we might watch a porn so we phoned the porn man with our selection from the binder of choices. He switched it on from somewhere and the porn started playing, but everyone's privates were blurred out so I kept doing this thing of trying to see around the circle of blur but of course I couldn't. So we decided we should hurry and have sex because you paid for the room by the minute and not day so us lying on a bed for the first time since arriving in Japan and touching and kissing stroke and stroke and no, nothing. And touch and lick and kiss and touch and touch and no, nothing. And you all sheepish and me cranky not because we couldn't, but because I wouldn't want to even if we could and us putting our clothes back on and phoning the porn man and telling him to send us the bill. And after a few seconds, we heard *shhhhhhhhh*-wop. This canister has come sucking through this tube with our bill in it. 'Cool,' I said. 'Like 1984.' So you paid in cash and put the canister back into the piping. I couldn't believe it. 'Do you want to keep a towel or the bathrobe or something?' you asked, and I said, 'Naw, it's okay.' So we left the room and went back to the car, never seeing a single soul, and drove back to your parents' house."

"Funny, how you remember things like that," he said.

"Yeah, I don't know why."

"What brought this on?"

"I don't know. Something anyways."

"Do you feel better now?"

"Yes. Thank you."

Stinky Girl

One is never certain when one becomes a stinky girl. I am almost positive I wasn't stinky when I slid out from between my mother's legs, fresh as blood and just as sweet. What could be stinkier, messier, grosser than that? one might be asked. But I'm certain I must have smelled rich, like yeast and liver. Not the stink of I-don't-know-what which pervades me now.

Mother has looked over my shoulder to see what I am trying to cover up with my hand and arm, while I meditatively write at the kitchen table.

"Jesus!" she rolls her eyes like a whale. "Jesus Christ!" she yells. "Don't talk about yourself as 'one'! One what, for God's sake? One asshole? One snivelling stinky girl?" She stomps off. Thank goodness. It's very difficult having a mother. It's even more difficult having a loud and coarse one.

Where was I? Oh yes. I am not troubled by many things. My size, my mother, my dead father's ghost, and a pet dog that despises me do not bother me so very much. Well, perhaps on an off day, they might bring a few tears to my eyes, but no one will notice a fat stinky mall rat weeping. People generally believe that fatties secrete all sorts of noxious substances from their bodies. But regardless. The one bane of my life, the one cloud of doom which circumscribes my life is the odour of myself.

35

There's no trying to pinpoint it. The usual sniff under the armpits or cupping of palms in front of my mouth to catch the smell of my breath is like trying to scoop an iceberg with a goldfish net. And it's not a simple condition of typical body odour. I mean, everybody has natural scents and even the prettiest cover girls wear deodorant and perfume. It's not the fact that I am fat that foul odours are trapped in the folds of my body. No, my problem is not a causal phenomenon and there are no simple answers.

Perhaps I am misleading, calling myself a mall rat. It's true I spend much of my time wandering in the subculture of gross material consumerism. I meander from store to store in the wake of my odour, but I seldom purchase anything I see inside the malls. Think, if you will, upon the word "rat." Instantly, you'll see a sharp-whiskered nose, beady black eyes, and an unsavoury disposition. Grubby hands with dirty fingernails, perhaps, and a waxy tail. You never actually, think, FAT RAT. No, I'm sure what comes to mind is a more sneaky and thinner rodent. If I am a rat, think of, perhaps, the queen of all rats in the sewer of her dreams, being fed the most tender morsels of garbage flesh her minions bring her. Think of a well-fed rat with three mighty chins and smooth, smooth skin, pink and fine. No need for a fur covering when all your needs are met. A mighty rodent with more belly than breath, more girth than the diameter of the septic drains. If you think of such a rat, then I am that mighty beast.

Actually, I had always thought of myself more in terms of a vole or perhaps a wise fat toad, or maybe even a manatee, mistaken by superstitious sailors as a bewitching mermaid. But, no. My mother tells me I was born in the Year of the Rat and that is that. No choice there, I'm afraid, and I can't argue with what I can't remember. Mother isn't one for prolonged arguments and contemplative discussions. More often than not, all I'll get is a "Jesus Christ!" for all my intellectual and moral efforts. I hope I don't sound judgmental. Mother is a creature unto herself and there is no ground for arbitrary comparison. Each to their own is a common phrase, but not without a tidbit of truth.

Perhaps I mislead you, calling myself a stinky girl. I am not a girl in the commonly held chronological sense of time. I've existed outside my mother's body for three and thirty years. Some might even go as far as to say that I'm an emotionally crippled and mutually dependent member of a dysfunctional family. Let's not quibble. In the measure of myself, and my sense of who I am, I am definitely a girl. Albeit, a stinky one.

When people see obesity, they are amazed. Fascinated. Attracted and repulsed simultaneously. Now if we could harness all the emotions my scale inspires, who knows how many homes it would heat, how many trains it would move? People always think there is a reason behind being grand. That there must be some sort of glandular problem, or an eating disorder, a symptom of some childhood trauma. All I can say is: not to my knowledge. I have always been fat, and, if I must say so myself, I eat a lot less than my tiny mother. I wasn't adopted, either. Mother is always bringing up how painful her labour was as she ejected me from her body. How she had to be tied down and how she pushed and screamed and pushed and cursed for three days running. Perhaps that's the reason for her slightly antagonistic demeanour. She didn't have any more children after I was born, and I must say, this birthing thing sounds like an unpleasant business. What with all the tying down and screaming.

Oh, yes. I do have siblings but they are much older than I. Three sisters and a brother who became women and a man long before their due. Cherry was born in the Year of the Rabbit; Ginger, the Year of the Dragon; Sushi, the Year of the Horse; Bonus, the Year of the Sheep. Mother was feeling quite tired of the whole affair by the time her second last child was born. Bonus was so named because he came out of her body with such ease she couldn't believe her luck. There was a seventeen-year stretch with no other pregnancies, and she must have thought that her cycles were finished. And what better way than to end on a bonus?

But Mother wasn't fated to an easy existence. She wasn't going to inhabit the autumn years of her life without considerable trials and tribulations. At the age of fifty-one, she became pregnant with me and promptly thereafter, my father died and she was left in a trailer, huge and growing, her children all moved away. A tragic life, really, but no. I shouldn't romanticize. One is easily led toward a tragic conclusion, and one must fight the natural human tendency to dramaticize the conditions of one's life. One must be level-headed. A fat girl especially. When one is fat, one is seldom seen as a stable and steadying force in an otherwise chaotic world. Fat people embody the disruptive forces in action and this inspires people to lay blame. Where else to point their fingers, but at the fat girl in striped trousers?

Did I mention I am also coloured?

I can't remember my very first memory. No one can, of course. But I must remember what others have told me before I could remember on my own. Of my living father I have no recollections. But his ghost is all too present in my daily life. I wouldn't be one to complain if he was a helpful and cheerful ghost, prone to telling me where there are hidden crocks of gold or if the weather will be fine for the picnic. But no. He is a dreadfully doleful one, following me around the small spaces in our trailer, leaning mournfully on my shoulder and telling me to watch my step *after* I've stepped in a pile of dog excrement. And such a pitiful apparition! All that there is of him is his

sad and sorry face. Just his head, bobbing around in the air, sometimes at the level of a man walking, but more often than not down
around the ankles, weaving heavily around one's steps. It's enough
to make one want to kick him, but I am not one who is compelled to
exhibit unseemly aggressive behaviour.

Mother, on the other hand, is not above a swift "kick in the can,"
as she calls it, or a sudden cuff to the back of the head. I would not
be exaggerating if I said I had no idea how she can reach my buttocks, let alone reach high enough to cuff my head, for I am not only
very fat, but big and tall all around. Well, tall might be misleading. It
would make one imagine that length is greater than girth. Let there
be no doubt as to my being rounder than I would ever be considered
tall. Only that I am at least a foot and a half taller than my mother,
who stands four foot eight. Medically speaking, she is not a dwarf,
and I am not a giant. But we are not normal in the commonly held
sense of the word.

No, my mother is not a dwarf, but she is the centre of the uni-
verse. Well, at least the centre of this trailer park, and she leaves no
doubt as to who "kicks the cabbage around this joint," as she is so
fond of reminding me. It gives me quite a chuckle on occasion, because father's ghost often looks much like a cabbage, rolling around
the gritty floor of our trailer, and even though Mother cannot see
him, she has booted his head many times, when she punctuates her
sayings with savage kicks to what she can only see as empty air. It
doesn't hurt him, of course, but it does seem uncomfortable. He rolls
his sorry eyes as he is tha-klunked tha-klunked across the kitchen.

"What are you sniggling at, Mall Rat?" Mother snaps at me.

"Nothing," I say, sniggling so hard that my body ripples like tides.

Mother kicks me in the can for lying and stomps off to her bedroom to smoke her cigars. I feel sorry for my father and right his
head, brush off some ghostly dust.

"See what happens when you inhabit this worldly prison? Why don't you float up to the heavens or at least a waiting room," I scold. "There's nothing left for you here except kicks in the head and a daughter who doesn't want to hear your depressing talk of dog excrement and all the pains you still feel in your phantom body that isn't there."

"As if I'm here by choice!" he moans. "As if any ghost would choose to remain in this purgatory excuse of a trailer! Finally dead and I get the nice light show, the tunnel thing, and a lovely floating body. I think that I might be hearing a chorus of singing mermaids when an unsympathetic voice bellows, 'You have not finished your time,' and I find my head bobbing in a yellow-stained toilet bowl. It takes me a couple of minutes to figure out it's my own toilet bowl in my old washroom, because I'd never seen the bathroom from that perspective before. Imagine my shock! What's a poor ghost to do? Oh woe, oh woe," he sobs. Because ghosts have ghostly licence to say things like that.

Frankly, his lamenting and woeing is terribly depressing, and I have plenty of my own woes without having to deal with his. I might not give in to excessive displays of violence, but I am not above stuffing him in the flour bin to make my escape.

I suppose calling oneself a rat might seem gender-specific. "Rat," I'll say, and instantly a man or a nasty boy is conjured up. There are female rats as well, don't you know. His and hers rat towels. Rat breasts and rat wombs. Rat washrooms where you squat instead of peeing standing. A girl can grow up to become a doctor or a lawyer now. Why not become a rat? Albeit, a stinky one.

Yes, yes, the odour of my life. It is large as myth and uglier than truth.

There are many unpleasant scents as you twiddle twaddle down the gray felt tunnels of life. Actually, smells hinge the past to the clutter of present memory. Nothing is comparable to the olfactory in terms of distorting your life. To jar a missing thought. Or transmute into an obsession. The dog excrement smell that's trapped in the runnels of the bottom of a sneaker, following you around all day no matter how fast you flee. That high-pitched whine of dog shit, pardon my language. Mother is a terrible influence and one must always guard against common usage and base displays of aggression. Yes, there is nothing like stepping in a pile of doggy dung to ruin your entire day. It is especially bad when the dog is supposedly your own.

Mother found the dog in the trailer park dumpster and as it was close to my "sorry birthday," as she called it, she brought the dirt-coloured, wall-eyed creature as a gift to me. I was touched, really, because she had forgotten to give me a gift for the last twenty-seven years and I had always wanted a dog as a devoted friend.

The dog started whining as soon as Mother dragged it into the trailer by the scruff of its mangy neck. It cringed on the floor, curling its lip back three times over. The dog started chasing itself, tried to catch up with its stumpy tail so it could eat itself out of existence. I was concerned.

"Mother, perhaps the dog has rabies."

"Arrghh." (This is the closest I can get in writing to the sound of my mother's laughter.) "Damn dog's not rabid, it's going crazy from your infernal stink. Lookit! It's hyperventilating! Aaaaaarrggghhh!"

The poor beast was frothing, chest heaving, smearing itself into the kitchen linoleum. It gave a sudden convulsive shake, then fainted. It was the first time I ever saw a dog faint. Needless to say, my "sorry birthday" was ruined. I actually thought the dog would die, or at least flee from my home as soon as it regained conscious-ness. But surprisingly, the animal stayed. There is no accounting for dog sense. Perhaps it's a puerile addiction to horrible smells. Like after one has cut up some slightly-going-off ocean fish and raises one's fishy fingers to one's nostrils throughout the day and night until the smell has been totally inhaled. Or sitting down in a chair and crossing an ankle over the knee, clutching the ankle with a hand, twisting so the bottom of the runner is facing upward. The nose descends to sniff, sniff, sniff again. There is an unborn addict in all of us, and it often reveals itself in the things we choose to smell.

I must admit, I cannot smell myself because I have smelled my scent into normality. I only know that I still emit a tremendous odour because my mother tells me so, I have no friends, and people give me a wide berth when I take my trips to the mall. There is a certain look people cannot control when they smell an awful stink. The lips curl back, the nose wrinkles toward the forehead, trying to close itself. (Actually, if one thinks about it, the nostrils seem more greatly exposed when in this position than at rest, but I needn't linger on that thought just now. Later, I'll ponder it at my leisure.) People cannot control this reaction. I have seen it the whole of my life and can interpret the fine sneer in the corner of an eye, a cheek twitching with the sudden sour bile rising from the bottom of the tongue.

Let me reassure you, I am not some obsessive fecal compulsive who is actually pleasured by excrement and foul odours. I am not in the league of people who get perverted thrills from the filth of metabolic processes. I bathe twice a day, despite the discomfort of squeezing my body into a tiny shower stall. Not to mention all the commotion Mother makes about how much hot water I use. I must say, though, that Mother would be wise to take greater care with her personal hygiene, what with her cigars and her general disregard for appearance and decorum.

In the summertime, I can bathe myself in my shower garden. I planted a hedge of caragana for some privacy and I only clip it width-wise, so it doesn't invade the yard. The foliage stands over ten feet in height and inside the scratchy walls, when it is heady with yellow blossoms, I can stand beneath an icy stream of hose water and almost feel beautiful. Mother always threatens to burn my beautiful bush to the ground.

"Like a damn scrub prison in here! Get no bloody sunlight in the yard. Nothing grows. Just mud and fungus and you muck it up with water and wallow there like some kind of pig. Burn the thing to the ground," she smacks me with her words. But Mother isn't as cruel as her words may sometimes seem. She does not reveal her inner spirit to those who are looking. Instead, she heaps verbal daggers in order not to be seen. Regardless, I know she will never burn down my summer shower, because sometimes I catch her standing inside the bower of caragana. All summer long. When the days are summer long into night and the heat is unbearable, the humble yellow blossoms turn into brittle brown pods. The shells crack with tiny explosions of minute seeds that bounce and scatter on the parched ground. They roll to where my mother douses herself with icy water. I catch her when she thinks I'm still at the mall. I catch her hosing her scrawny old woman body, a smile on her scowl face, cigar burning between her lips. I never let on I see her in these moments. She is more vulnerable than I.

The dog decided to remain in the confines of our trailer and I realized one can never foretell the life choices that others will enact. Mother called him Rabies, and dragged his floppy body outside. She hosed him off in the caragana shower and he came to, shook himself off as dogs will do, slunk into the kitchen, and hunkered beneath the table. Mother laughed once: "Aaarrrrrgh," and threw him the first thing her hand came in contact with inside the refrigerator.

It was Father's head.

I had tucked him there to keep him from being underfoot, and he must have fallen asleep. The starving dog clamped down on an ear and gnawed with stumpy teeth. Father screamed with outrage.

"What you say, Stink-O? Speak up. Fat girls shouldn't whisper."

"Nothing, Mother. I think you tossed Rabies a cabbage. I'll just take it back and feed him something more suitable. Perhaps that beef knuckle we used to make soup yesterday."

"Suit yourself. But don't say, 'perhaps'." Mother stomped off "to sit on the can," as she calls it.

"A dog," Father moaned. "Your mother fed me to a dog. Haven't I been tormented enough? When will this suffering end?" He started weeping, the dog keening. I sighed. I am not one who gives in easily to the woes of this world. Sighing is an expression of defeat, or at least weakness, which reveals a lack of worldly toughness or a certain get-up-and-go attitude. But Father is a sorry shade, a cloud of perpetual doom and defeat. I don't even want to know what sort of man he was before he had fallen to this. It would only make a tragic comedy out of what was probably a pathetic life. I swooped down, scooped Father's head from between Rabies' paws, and set him on the table, right side up. Dug through the garbage for the dry soup bone and tossed it to the dog.

Yes, a fat girl can swoop. I am remarkably light on my feet, I almost float on the tips of my toes. Certainly, one may be fat and stinky, but it doesn't necessitate stumbling awkwardness. I never drag my feet and I never stomp, fit to bring down the roof. It is Mother who is the stomper in this house and many a time I have whipped up the ladder to tap another layer of tarry paper on the rusty roof. I may be grand, stink, and be hated by dogs, but I have a dancer's feet and the endurance of a rice-planter's thighs.

44

Did I mention that I'm also coloured? One is led to say "also" in a long list of things I am that are not commonly perceived as complimentary. One cannot say, "I'm coloured," and expect, "You know, I've always wanted to be coloured myself," as a standard reaction. Not that I would rather be a stinky, fat, white girl. Perhaps, mauve or plum. Plum . . . now that's a colour!

A fat coloured rat girl has to look out for herself and never reveal her cards. Lucky for me, I must say I'm blessed with a certain higher intelligence, a certain sensitivity which enables me to more than endure the trials of this existence. On my better days, I can leap and soar above the tarry roof of the trailer house. On my better days, the stars sing closer to my ears. I may be fat, I may stink larger than life, I may be a coloured mall rat in striped trousers, but I am coyly so.

Ah, yes, the mall. Now why would such a clever girl as myself bother to habit such a gross manifestation of consumer greed? Is it some puerile addiction, a dysfunction I cannot control? Many a time I've pondered on this, but it is not as an active consumer I return to the mall as I oft do. My forays there are part of an ongoing study of the plight of human existence in a modern colonized country. A mall is the microcosm, the centrifugal force in a cold country where much of the year is sub-zero in temperature. The mall reveals the dynamics of the surrounding inhabitants. Yes, the habits of the masses can be revealed in the Hudson's Bay department store and in the vast expanses of a Toys 'R' Us where hideously greedy children manipulate TV dinner divorcees into making purchases with the monetary equivalence to feeding a small village for a week.

When I have fully understood the human mall condition, it will become a doorway to a higher level of existence. One must understand one's limitations, the shackles of social norms, in order to overcome them. And when I have accomplished this, I will cast aside my mantle of foul odour and float to the outer limits of time and space. Alas, one must always have a care not to steep oneself too deeply in theoretical thought. It would only lead to the sin created by the Greeks and taught in every Western educational institution today. Hubris, dreaded hubris.

Luckily for me, my father's pale and pathetic head is confined to the parameters of our trailer lot. Imagine what a hindrance he'd be in my pursuit of higher consciousness! I slip into my gymnast's slippers and *chassé* through my caragana bowers and out the tattered gate. Father's head rolls down the walk after me as far as the last concrete slab, then teeters back and forth in what I assume is a head wave. Feeling extra generous, I throw back a kiss. And he levitates a few feet in pleasure. There is no sight nor sound of Rabies, much to my father's relief.

"Arrr! Stink-O!" Mother snarls from the tiny bathroom window. "Pick me up a box of cigars. Don't cheap out on me and buy those candy-flavoured Colts, you hear!" I blow kisses, five, six, seven, and flutter down the sidewalk. Mother, or her bowels, growl from the dark recesses of our tinny home.

As I traipse between the rows of identical rectangular homes festooned with painted plywood butterflies and plastic petunias, I hear the slamming of doors and the snap of windows being closed. My odour precedes me and I never need an introduction. My signature prevails. Alas, a thought. If one smells a smell and was never taught to like it, would one not find it distasteful as a result of ignorance? Let me pursue the opposite line of thought. If one were taught as a very small child that roses were disgusting, that they were vilely noxious and ugly to boot, would one not despise the very thought of their scent? It may be that I smell beautiful beyond the capacity of human recognition. The scent of angels and salamanders. And no one to appreciate the loveliness before their very senses.

The mall. The mall. The Saturday mall is a virtual hub of hustle and bustle. Crying infants and old women smoking. Unisex teens sprouting rings from every inch of revealed skin and the mind boggles thinking about what's not revealed. Fake and real potatos French fried into greasy sticks, stand-in-line Chinese food, trendy café au laits and iced coffees. It is crowded but I always have a wide path to myself. A minimum three-metre radius circumscribes my epicentre. No one dares breach this space, I'm afraid. Like a diver in a shark cage. No, that's not quite right. Regardless.

I have a daily route I take and even if my eyes were put out, I could wind my way through the blind corners and dead end halls of this mall. Like the tragic Shakespearean kings, I would prevail with an uncanny sense of despair and enlightenment. The merchants all know me by smell, and sometimes a wave or a brief nod of a head is offered. There was a time when most of the merchants had convened to try to put an end to my forays. To banish me from my chosen road of human contemplation. But legally there was nothing they could do as long as I bought an item now and again, like Mother's cigars, or a soup bone from the butcher. They couldn't evict me for the way I smell, or how I look in my striped trousers. There was a time when I could have been evicted for being coloured, but at this present time in history, and in this geographical location, I am lawfully tolerated.

Alas, no one wants to be merely tolerated, like a whining child or an ugly dog. Such human arrogance. We dare assume that some are meant to be merely tolerated while others are sought out to be idolized, glorified, even to wipe their dainty asses. Have a care! I mustn't fall into the pit of baseness like my mother before me! The utter unfairness of it all is enough to make one want to bite one's own tongue off, a mute supplication to the evils of this world, but that's the other end of the stick. Father's end of misery and woe. It is my chosen path to seek another. . . .

I glide into Holy Smoke to pick out a box of cigars for Mother. If I wait until I have done my daily study of the machinations of mall existence, I may very well forget and Mother would be sorely vexed. In a manner which would be audible for several square kilometres.

"Good afternoon," Adib nods politely from behind his pastel handkerchief.

"Lovely," I breezily smile. Step up to the marble counter.

"A box of the usual for you?" He backs up a pace, crinkling his eyes into smiles, to make up for his instinctual retreat.

"Please," I bob and lean my arm against the cool grey rock slab that runs the length of the entire store. Men on stools on either side of me hop off, stuff burning pipes in trouser pockets in their haste to escape me. Adib sighs, even though he has his back to the mass exodus. He turns around with a box filled with cigars as thick as my thumb, individually wrapped and sealed with a red sticker. He has thrown five extra ones on top, so my return will take a little longer.

"Your generosity is so greatly appreciated," I bow, clicking my heels like some military personage and pay him with bills sweating wetly from the pocket of my striped pants.

Adib accepts them as graciously as a man extending a pair of tweezers can. No, I am not angered by his reticence to come into direct contact with me. Indeed, I find his manner refreshingly honest and he never hurls abuse like some opt to do.

"My best to your mother," Adib nods, handing me my change via tweezers. "By the way," he adds, "you might want to take in the new children's play area in the western wing of the mall. I hear that it's quite the development."

"Why, thank you," I beam. Then frown. "But how is it that I am not acquainted with this wonder of childish bliss?"

Adib just shrugs, breathing shallowly from behind his scented lavender hanky. I thank him again. *Glissande en avant* through the door and, toes pointed, leap excitedly to the west wing.

The sign reads: FRIENDZIES!

It's one of those obscure word conflations that mean almost nothing at all. Like a joke told with a punch line from another, one realizes there is an attempt at humour, but there is nothing to get. It does not bode well.

Grand opening balloons, limp and wrinkled, dangle from pastel walls. Streamers trail limply from golden pillars, curling in the dust on the cold floor. A table with free coffee and donuts and Coke-flavoured pop made out of syrup. I walk up to the gate, disheartened, but must enter for study purposes. One must not let first impressions alter one's methodology, one's code of conduct.

"One adult, please," I smile courteously.

"Where's your kid?" a girl asks, chewing an unseemly quantity of gum.

I am amazed. She does not curl her nose in disgust from the stench that permeates from my being. Her eyes do not water and she doesn't gape at my size.

"I have no children," I say, "I just want to view the newly constructed premises." How is it that she doesn't seem to notice? Perhaps her nose has been decimated from smoking or, perhaps, lines of cocaine.

"Ya can't go in without a kid, because adults go in free, but a kid costs eight bucks." The girl tips forward on her stool to rest her chin in her hands, elbows sloppily on the countertop before me.

"My goodness! Eight dollars for a child!" I am shocked. Who could afford to entertain their children here?

"What if one were to tell you that the child is inside already, that one has only to come to join her?"

The young woman kicks a button with her foot and the gate swings open. "Don't forget to take off your shoes and keep valuables on your person," she intones, rote and bored to insensibility.

She is from a generation where nothing seems to matter. She is so bored of the world and of herself that even my anomalous presence doesn't measure on her radar. Is there no hope for our next generation? Will the non-starving members of our species perish from ennui even before we've polluted our environment to the point of no return?

This turn of thought does nothing to advance my research. It only makes me weary. Ever weary. I adjust my mental clipboard and focus on the task at hand.

Plastic tubing runs crazily throughout the room, like a diseased mind twisting, turning back on itself with no end, no beginning. Plastic balls fill a pit of doom, three toddlers drowning to the chorus of their parents' snap-shotting delight. Primary reds, blues, and yellows clash horribly with khaki, lavender, and peach. Children, fat children, skinny children, coloured children pale from too much TV, run half-heartedly through the plastic pipes, their stocking feet pad-padding in the tubes above my head. They squeal listlessly from expectation rather than delight. A playground for children constructed from a culture of decay. There is enough plastic here to make Tupperware for an entire continent and I am too stunned to gape in horrified dismay.

Mother would think this a grandiose joke. Would laugh in her cigar-breath way, her ever-present stogie clenched between her molars in a manner that would make Clint Eastwood envious. Mother would enjoy this place to no end, but I am stricken. I am an urban rat, but I still recognise the forces of the sun, the moon, the patterns of wind that guide me. Albeit, through a film of pollution. These tragic children who are taught to play in an artificial world can only follow the route to an artificial death. Their spirits will be trapped forever with a shelf-life of an eternity.

I wander, dazed, dismayed, my dancer's feet dragging heavily on the Astroturf. Some of the older, anemic children stop and stare, whisper to each other from behind covered mouths. I take no heed. I continue through the cultural maze of hyper-artificiality.

There is no hope, my mind mutters incessantly. My steps slow, motion stilled, all joie de vivre leached through the bottom of my feet.

Stone.

A toddler topples backward out of chute. A millisecond of silence. Then she bawls like the world has ended. Red, yellow, and blue balls fly fitfully through the air. Children gulp from tubs of simulated Coke while waiting for their microwave-heated pizzas. A boy bends over and plat! Vomits a soft pink mound of hotdogs.

Horrible humanity. How can I bear this?

How can anyone bear it?

No! I must not waver from my calling. I will not follow the path of my father into woe and I won't encrust my airy spirit within a coarse mantle like my mother. It is not enough to simply stand on the outside and gape, albeit with a closed mouth. It is not enough that only I fully understand the human mall condition. What if I *am* to overcome the shackles of social norms and thus, reach the outer limits of time and space? Do I want to survey the vista, alone? I must join the epicentre of humanity.

I must enter the maze.

"Watch your fat can," I can hear my mother's raspy voice all around me. "Don't come crying to me. I'll only say 'I told you so,' and kick you in the butt."

Mother, oh Mother.

I circle the strange man-made maze, thinking to myself that a woman never would. Circle thrice before I spot a young child scurrying up a hot pink pipe, like a rabbit with a watch. I adjust my mental clipboard and squelch my body into the mouth of the tube, wishing for a ball of thread.

Fat rat in a sewer pipe. The thought bubbles hysterically to the surface of my mind, but I kick it in the can in the manner of my mother.

What is interesting is that instead of getting stuck like an egg in the throat of an over-greedy snake, my body elongates. Spreads towards the ends so that all I need to do is flutter my toes to initiate a forward motion.

I slide, glide smoothly through the twisting tubing. The only impediments are the large metal heads of bolts that are used to fasten the portions of pipe together. The friction of clothing against the plastic raises such electricity that I am periodically zapped with great sparks and frazzle. Definitely a design flaw. Children in neighbouring tubes pad, pad, twirl down spiral slides. Their small muffled noises are only broken with intermittent zaps and small exclamations of pain.

I have never cared for children although I've cared about them in theory. . . .

Something pokes the bottom of my foot. Of course, I cannot turn around to look. A barely discernible voice squeaks in protest and the single voice is joined with another, another. For in my contemplation I've ceased my inching progress and I've blocked the tube like a clot of fat in an artery. Their small mouse-like rustlings unsettle my philosophical and scientific musings. I would wave them away if I could face them, but all I do is flap my foot in a discouraging manner.

Then I notice. A certain *something*. For the first time in my life, that which has always been with me yet never perceived seeps into my consciousness. I am so completely encased in plastic that it cannot be diluted by outer forces.

I can smell myself.

But the wonder!

Because my odour is not smell, but sound. . . .

The unbearable voices of mythic manatees, the cry of the phoenix, the whispers of kappa lovers beside a gurgling stream. The voice of the moon that is ever turned from our gaze, the song of suns colliding. The sounds that emanate from my skin are so intense that mortal senses recoil, deflect beauty into ugliness as a way of coping. Unable to bear hearing such unearthly sounds they transmute it into stench.

And my joy! Such incredible joy. The hairs on my arms stand electric, the static energy and my smell/sound mix such dizzying intensity the plastic surrounding me bursts apart, falls away from my being like an artificial cocoon.

I hover, twenty feet in the air.

The children who were stuck behind me tumble to the ground. They fall silently, too shocked to scream, but the pitch of sound that seeps from my skin intensifies, like beams of coloured light. The sound catches the children from their downward plummet and they bob, rise slowly up to where I float. I extend my hands and the children grab hold, hold each others' hands, smile with wonder.

"Oh my god!" someone finally gasps, from far beneath us. Another person screams. Fathers faint and an enterprising teenager grabs a camera from a supine parent and begins to snap pictures. None of it matters. This moment. Tears drip from my eyes and the liquid jewels float alongside us like diamonds in outer space. I burst out laughing and the children laugh too. I don't know what will happen tomorrow or the day that follows but the possibilities are immeasurable.

We float, the remaining plastic pipes shimmer, buckle beneath our voices, then burst into soft confetti.

Tales From the Breast

The questions that were never asked may be the most important. You don't think of this. You never do. When you were little, your mother used to tell you that asking too many questions could get you into trouble. You realize now that not asking enough has landed you in the same boat, in the same river of shit without the same paddle. You phone your mother long distance to tell her this and she says, "Well, two wrongs don't make a right, dear," and gives you a dessert recipe that is reported as being Prince Charles's favourite in the September issue of *Royalty* magazine.

Your Child's First Journey, page 173:
Your success in breastfeeding depends greatly on your desire to nurse as well as the encouragement you receive from those around you.

"Is there anything coming out?" He peers curiously at the baby's head, my covered breast.

"I don't know, I can't tell," I wince.

"What do you mean, you can't tell? It's your body, isn't it? I mean, you must be able to feel something," scratching his head.

"Nope, only pain."

"Oh." Blinks twice. "I'm sorry. I'm very proud of you, you know."

The placenta slips out from between your legs like the hugest blood clot of your life. The still-wet baby is strong enough to nurse but cannot stagger to her feet like a fawn or a colt. You will have to carry her in your arms for a long time. You console yourself with the fact that at least you are not an elephant who would be pregnant for close to another year. This is the first and last time she will nurse for the next twelve hours.

"Nurse, could you please come help me wake her up? She hasn't breastfed for five hours now."

The nurse has a mole with a hair on it. You can't help but look at it a little too long each time you glance up at her face. She undresses the baby but leaves the toque on. The infant is red and squirmy and you hope no one who visits says she looks just like you.

"Baby's just too comfortable," the nurse chirps. "And sometimes they're extra tired after the delivery. It's hard work for them too, you know!"

"Yeah, I suppose you're right."

"Of course. Oh, and when you go to the washroom, I wouldn't leave Baby by herself. Especially if the door is open." The nurse briskly rubs the red baby until she starts squirming, eyes still closed in determined sleep.

"What do you mean?"

"Well, we have security, but really, anyone could just waltz in and leave with Baby." The nurse smiles, like she's joking.

"Are you serious?"

"Oh, yes. And you shouldn't leave valuables around, either. We've been having problems with theft, and I know you people have nice cameras."

You have endured twelve hours of labour and gone without sleep for twenty-eight. You do not have the energy to tell the nurse of the inappropriateness of her comment. The baby does not wake up.

Your mother-in-law, from Japan, has come to visit. She is staying for a month to help with the older child. She gazes at the sleeping infant you hold to your chest. You tell her that the baby won't feed properly and that you are getting a little worried.

"Your nipples are too flat and she's not very good at breastfeeding," she says, and angry tears fill your eyes.

"Are you people from Tibet?" the nurse asks.

Page 174:

Breastmilk is raw and fresh.

You are at home. You had asked if you could stay longer in the hospital if you paid, but they just laughed and said no. Your mother-in-law makes lunch for herself and the firstborn but does not make any for you because she does not know if you will like it. You eat shredded wheat with Nutra-sweet and try breastfeeding again.

The pain is raw and fresh.

She breastfeeds for three hours straight, and when you burp her, there is a pinkish froth in the corners of her lips that looks like strawberry milkshake. You realize your breast milk is blood-flavoured and wonder if it is okay for her to drink. Secretly, you hope that it is bad for her so that you will have to quit breastfeeding. When you call a friend and tell her about the pain and blood and your concerns for the baby's health, you learn, to your dismay, that the blood will not hurt her. That your friend had problems too, that she even had blood blisters on her nipples, but she kept right on breastfeeding through it, the doctor okayed it and ohhhh the blood, the pain, when those blood blisters popped, but she went right on breastfeeding until the child was four years old.

When you hang up, you are even more depressed. Because the blood is not a problem and your friend suffered even more than you do now. You don't come in first on the tragic nipple story. You don't even come close.

"This isn't going very well." I try smiling, but give up the effort.

"Just give it some time. Things'll get better." He snaps off the reading light at the head of the bed. I snap it back on.

"I don't think so. I don't think *things* are going to get better at all."

"Don't be so pessimistic," he smiles, trying not to offend me.

"Have you read the pamphlet for fathers of breastfed babies?"

"Uhhhhm, no. Not yet." Shrugs his shoulders and tries reaching for the lamp again. I swing out my hand to catch his wrist in midair.

"Well, read the damn thing and you might have some idea of what I'm going through."

"Women have been breastfeeding since there have been women."

"What!"

"You know what I mean. It's natural. Women have been breastfeeding ever since their existence, ever since ever having a baby," he lectures, glancing down once at my tortured breasts.

"That doesn't mean they've all been enjoying it, ever since existing and having done it since their existence! Natural isn't the same as liking it or being good at it," I hiss.

"Why do you have to be so complicated?"

58

"Why don't you just marry someone who isn't, then?"

"Are you hungry?" My mother-in-law whispers from the other side of the closed bedroom door. "I could fix you something if you're hungry."

Page 183:

Engorgement

The baby breastfeeds for hours on end. This is not the way the manual reads. You phone the emergency breastfeeding number they gave to you at the hospital. The breastfeeding professionals tell you that Baby is only doing what is natural. That the more she sucks, the more breast milk you will produce, how it works on a supply and demand system and how everything will be better when the milk comes in. On what kind of truck, you wonder.

They tell you that if you are experiencing pain of the nipples, it's because Baby isn't latched on properly. How the latch has to be just right for proper nursing. You don't like the sounds of that. You don't like how *latch* sounds like something that's suctioned on and might never come off again. You think of lamprey eels and leeches. Notice how everything starts with an "l".

When the milk comes in, it comes in on a semi-trailer. There are even marbles of milk under the surface of the skin in your armpits, hard as glass and painful to the touch. Your breasts are as solid as concrete balls and the pressure is so great that the veins around the nipple are swollen, bulging. Like the stuff of horror movies, they are ridged, expanded to the point of blood splatter explosion.

"Feel this, feel how hard my breasts are," I say, gritting my teeth.

"Oh my god!"

"It hurts," I whisper.

"Oh my god." He is horrified. Not with me, but at me.

"Can you suck them a little, so they're not so full? I can't go to sleep."

"What!" He looks at me like I've asked him to suck from a vial of cobra venom.

"Could you please suck some out? It doesn't taste bad. It's kinda like sugar water."

"Uhhh, I don't think so. It's so . . . incestuous."

"We're married, for god's sake, not blood relations. How can it be incestuous? Don't be so weird about it. Please! It's very painful."

"I'm sorry. I just can't." Clicks off the lamp and turns over to sleep.

Page 176:

*Advantages also exist for you, the nursing mother . . . it is easy for you to lose weight without dieting and **regain your shape sooner**.*

"You look like you're still pregnant," he jokes. "Are you sure there isn't another one still in there?"

"Just fuck off, okay?"

Your belly has a loose fold of skin and fat that impedes the sight of your pubic hair. You have a beauty mark on your lower abdomen you haven't seen for five years. You wonder if you would have had a better chance at being slimmer if you had breastfed the first child. There is a dark stain that runs vertically over the skin of your belly, from the pubic mound to the belly button and almost in line with the bottom of your breasts. Perversely, you imagined it to be the marker for the doctor to slice if the delivery had gone bad. The stain isn't going away and you don't really care because, what with the flab and all, it doesn't much make a difference. You are hungry all the time from producing breast milk and eat three times as much as you normally would, therefore you don't lose weight at all.

"You should eat as much as you want," your mother-in-law says. She spoons another slice of eggplant onto your plate and your partner passes his over as well. The baby starts to wail from the bedroom and your mother-in-law rushes to pick her up.

"Don't cry," you hear her say. "Breast milk is coming right away."

You want to yell down the hall that you have a name and it isn't Breast-Milk.

You eat the eggplant.

Page 176:

The hormone prolactin, which causes the secretion of milk, helps you to feel "motherly."

Just how long can the pain last, you ask yourself. It is the eleventh day of nipple torture and maternal hell. You phone a friend and complain about the pain, the endless pain. Your friend says that some people experience so much pleasure from breastfeeding that they have orgasms. If that were the case, you say, you would do it until the kid was big enough to run away from you.

The middle-of-the-night feed is the longest and most painful part of the breastfeeding day. It lasts from two to six hours. You alternate from breast to breast, from an hour at each nipple dwindling down to a half hour, fifteen minutes, eight minutes, two, one, as your nipples get so sore that even the soft brush of the baby's bundling cloth is enough to make your toes squeeze up into fists of pain, tears streaming down your cheeks. You try thinking about orgasms as the slow tick tick of the clock prolongs your misery. You try thinking of s&m. The pain is so intense, so slicing real, that you are unable to think of it as pleasurable. You realize that you are not a masochist.

Page 176:

*Because you must sit down or lie down to nurse, **you are assured of getting the rest** you need postpartum.*

You can no longer sit to breastfeed. You try lying down to nurse her like a puppy, but the shape of your breasts are not suitable for this method. You prop her up on the back of the easy chair and feed her while standing. Her legs dangle but she is able to suck on your sore nipples. You consider hanging a sign on your back: The Milk Stand.

Your ass is killing you. You take a warm sitz bath because it helps for a little while, and you touch yourself in the water as carefully as you can. You feel several new nubs of flesh between your vagina and your rectum and hopefully imagine that you are growing a second, third, fourth clitoris. When you visit your doctor, you find out that they're only hemorrhoids.

"I'm quitting. I hate this."

"You've only been at it for two weeks. This is the worst part and it'll only get better from here on," he encourages. Smiles gently and tries to kiss me on my nose.

"I quit, I tell you. If I keep on doing this, I'll start hating the baby."

"You're only thinking about yourself," he accuses, pointing a finger at my chest. "Breastfeeding is the best for her and you're giving up, just like that. I thought you were tougher."

"Don't you guilt me! It's my goddamn body and I make my own decisions on what I will and will not do with it!"

"You always have to do what's best for yourself! What about my input? Don't I have a say on how we raise our baby?" he shouts, Mr Sensible and let's-talk-about-it-like-two-adults.

"Is everything alright?" his mother whispers from outside the closed bedroom door. "Is anybody hun-"

"We're fine! Just go to bed!" he yells.

The baby snorts, hiccups into an incredible wail. Nasal and distressed.

"Listen, it's me who has to breastfeed her, me who's getting up every two hours to have my nipples lacerated and sucked on till they bleed while you just snore away. You haven't even got up once in the middle of the night to change her goddamn diaper even as a token fucking gesture of support, so don't you tell me what I should do with my breasts. There's nothing wrong with formula. I was raised on formula. You were raised on formula. Our whole generation was raised on formula and we're fine. So just shut up about it. Just shut up. Because this isn't about you. This is about me!"

"If I could breastfeed, I would do it gladly!" he hisses. Flings the blankets back and stomps to the crib.

And I laugh. I laugh because the sucker said the words out loud.

3:27 AM. The baby has woken up. Your breasts are heavy with milk but you supplement her with formula. 5:15. You supplement her again and your breasts are so full, so tight, that they lie like marble on your chest. They are ready.

You change the baby's diapers and put her into the crib. In the low glow of the baby light, you can see her lips pursed around an imaginary nipple. She even sucks in her sleep. You sit on the bed, beside your partner, and unsnap the catches of the nursing bra. The pads are soaked and once the nipples are exposed, they spurt with sweet milk. The skin around your breasts stretches tighter than a drum, so tight that all you need is one little slice for the skin to part. Like a pressured zipper, it tears, spreading across the surface of your chest, directed by your fingers, tears in a complete circle around the entire breast.

There is no blood.

You lean slightly forward and the breast falls gently into your cupped hands. The flesh is a deep red and you wonder at its beauty, how flesh becomes food without you asking or even wanting it. You set the breast on your lap and slice your other breast. Two pulsing orbs still spurting breast milk. You gently tug the blankets down from the softly clenched fingers of your partner's sleep, unbutton his pyjamas, and fold them back so his chest is exposed. You stroke the hairless skin, then lift one breast, then the other, to lie on top of his flat penny nipples. The flesh of your breasts seeps into his skin, soft whisper of cells joining cells, your skin into his, tissue to tissue, the intimate melding before your eyes, your mouth an "o" of wonder and delight.

The unfamiliar weight of engorged breasts makes him stir, restless, a soft moan between parted lips. They are no longer spurting with milk, but they drip evenly, runnels down his sides. The cooling wet becomes uncomfortable and his eyelids flutter. Open. He focuses on my face peering down and blinks rapidly.

"What's wrong?" he asks, voice dry with sleep.

"Nothing. Not a thing. How do you feel?"

"Funny," he answers, perplexed. "My chest feels funny. I feel all achy. Maybe I'm coming down with something. My chest is wet! I'm bleeding!"

"Shhhhh. You'll wake the baby," I caution. Gently press my forefinger over his lips.

He was groggy with sleep, but he now he's wide awake. Sitting up. Looks down at his chest, his two engorged breasts. He looks at my face. Then back at his breasts.

"Oh my god," he moans.

"It's okay," I nurture him. "Don't worry. Everything is fine. Just do what comes naturally."

A sudden look of shock slams into his face and he reaches, panicked, with his hands to touch himself between his legs. When he feels himself intact, his eyes flit with relief only to be permanently replaced with bewilderment.

I smile. Beam in the dim glow of light. Turn on to my side and sleep sweetly, soundly.

Drift

Her okā-san was trying. Her mother tried hard until they hit a blizzard just past Banff.

"It's difficult to see, isn't it? Ha-ha," her mother laughed weakly.

"It's not bad," Megumi muttered. "I've driven lots worse."

"Your otō-san says that it's good to have someone's tail-lights in front so you can follow them, ha-ha."

Yah, right off a cliff, Megumi thought. She didn't say anything, but turned up the volume on her *Tank Girl* soundtrack.

"What's this kind of music? Did you bring anything else?"

"It's from a movie. I brought some enka and Okinawa folk songs for you."

"Oh? No classical?" Hisako reached for a Kleenex so she could twist it instead of clutching the door handle. "Do you let the children listen to this kind of music? She sounds like a chicken being strangled, ha-ha."

Megumi sniffed.

"I wonder if the children will be alright with Barney. He's so nice to watch them for you."

"They're his kids too. He's not watching them for me. He's watching them for himself." Megumi clicked her high beams at an asshole who hadn't dimmed his own.

"You're so ill-tempered. But you always were ill-tempered," Hisako said, sighing almost nostalgically. "Barney is very patient. He's very nice. But Barney, ha-ha. What a name for a grown man, ha-ha."

"Will you stop that?"

"Stop what?" her mother asked.

"Laughing that fake 'ha-ha'! It's not like you're really laughing. You think you can say anything and then, 'ha-ha,' after it and it will be okay!"

"You always get so mad no matter what I say. I won't say anything at all!" Hisako turned stiffly to stare out the chilled pane of glass.

Shit. Megumi had loved the song and now all that would run through her head was "chicken being strangled." Ha-ha.

God!

And hadn't any of the other drivers on the stinkin' highway seen snow before? What was wrong with them? It was Canada, for god's sake. The Rockies.

Three semi-trailers and an out-of-season camper crept in front of Megumi and she clenched the steering wheel, shoved her shoulders forward, and willed them to step on it. A good straight stretch. Megumi tromped on the accelerator and roared past the camper and hurled toward the first semi-truck.

Her mother screamed.

They stopped, fifteen kilometres later, in Golden.

"How are YA!" Megumi's father shouted after he accepted the collect call. She didn't know why he had to shout every time he got on the phone. Maybe it was an immigrant thing. Then again, maybe he was going deaf.

"We're in Golden," Megumi said sourly.

"Ha! Ha! HAAAA! I TOLD your okā-san you wouldn't get any farther than Revelstoke toNIGHT."

"We've had a fight already."

"See why we don't travel together anyMORE?!" her otō-san shouted.

"That's pathetic. Why don't you get a divorce, then, if you can't even stand to travel together?"

"I LOVE my HUNNY!"

God! Megumi rolled her eyes and handed the phone to her mom.

Hisako smiled and turned her back. "She just gets so angry. . . ."

Megumi could hear her father's tinny shout from the other side of her mother's head. "DON'T tell her HOW TO DRIVE! She HATES THAT THE MOST!"

"You hate that the most, ha-ha," Hisako laughed.

Megumi rolled her eyes. Flopped back on to the floral cover of the double bed she'd have to share with her mom.

"I love you too, Hunny," her okā-san smiled. Hisako hung up the phone, then passed it to her daughter.

"Aren't you going to call Barney and the children?"

"The kids are asleep already. I'll call tomorrow."

"Well, you could call Barney. . . ."

"Mom! I told you! We're SEPARATED! The last thing he wants is to TALK TO ME ON THE PHONE!"

"STOP YELLING AT ME!" Hisako shouted.

The wailing pitch of a newborn baby squalling awake and angry came from the other side of the wall. Megumi and her mom looked guiltily at each other.

"Sorry," they both muttered.

"Ha-ha," Hisako breathed.

The late-night Denny's 24-hour breakfast was a congealed ball of lard in Megumi's gut. She turned onto her side and burped hash browns. A couple of sour, grainy chunks rose up, but she swallowed them back down. Her okā-san had her butt sticking out of the side of the thin bed-cover. Thank god, Megumi thought. And burped again. Megumi knew that her mother was still awake, because she kept on farting. The clock radio glowed red. 2:47 AM. God. She should have made her sister come too, so that someone else could drive. How would she ever make it, the ferry to catch then that winding road with not enough sleep? Her mom screaming the whole way. What was she thinking?

"No fucking way I'm going to the mountains. It's cold. No fucking way I'm going to a slimy hot spring. Naked! Off a logging road! Don't you remember *Deliverance?*" Her sister lit another cigarette and blew stink into Megumi's face.

"It's perfectly safe. I've been there eight times. People who go there are into nature. The most they do is smoke dope. You can wear a swimsuit, you know."

"Why're you bothering to take her anywhere? I can't stand travelling with her. Especially when she does that passive aggressive shit."

"It's not all her fault the way she is."

"You're such a suck," her sister said. Waved her smoke. "No fucking way I'm going."

Megumi sighed. Hisako farted. 2:49 AM.

There was a thump. Then another. Thump. Thump. Bump. Bump. Thump bump. "Ah. Ah. Oh. Oh. Oh. Ah. Ah. Ahhhhh. AHHHHH. Ah."

"Oh dear," Hisako breathed.

Megumi giggled.

"They're having congress. And the baby's sleeping in the same room. . . ." Hisako whispered.

70

"Imagine," Megumi snorted.

"It might affect the child's psychological development. It might grow up to be over-sexed or, you know, strange. . . ."

"What are you implying?" Megumi prickled.

"Nothing! I'm saying, it's just wrong. Having congress in the same room with an innocent baby!"

"Okā-san, remember how my crib was in you and dad's room until I was three?"

"Yes. . . ."

"I saw you and dad doing it!"

"No! That's untrue!"

"I remember it clearly. I remember you piling on top of each other and pushing."

"Stop it!" Hisako shrieked.

Megumi laughed. "I thought you were wrestling."

Hisako sucked in her breath. "Then it's our fault that you – you're with that woman!"

Megumi breathed deep and exhaled slowly. "Okā-san, being a lesbian –"

"DON'T SAY THAT WORD!"

"Okā-san –"

"NO!"

"Alright. We don't have to talk about anything." Megumi curled tight around her middle. And sleep didn't come for many hours.

After a brief tussle over the motel bill, they hit the road without breakfast. They stopped in Revelstoke for the ferry schedule and a stretch. Megumi ordered some coffee and Hisako bought pumpkin seeds.

"You shouldn't use that fake sugar," her mother warned. "It makes you lose your faculties when you're older. Or causes brain cancer or something. Ha-ha."

"I know it's unhealthy," Megumi sighed. "But I like my coffee really sweet and I don't want to get any fatter."

"Your father thinks your sister went to fat because of the Pill, ha-ha."

"She's not fat. But it's true, the Pill affects your body in all sorts of ways. I mean, it causes your body to think it's pregnant, for god's sake."

They climbed back into their car, Hisako cracking pumpkin seeds and putting the husks in a Kleenex.

"Are you on the Pill?" she asked.

"Ummmm," Megumi glanced at her mother. Wondering what planet she came from. Or which biology class she missed. "I don't really need to be on it."

Silence.

Then crack, cracking of pumpkin seeds.

Megumi flicked a look again. Her okā-san's lips were pinched. There were bags beneath her eyes.

"You don't have to stay awake for me," Megumi said gently. "You can go to sleep. I'm not tired. And I promise not to pass anyone."

"I don't want to sleep," Hisako said, smiling. "I haven't had a holiday for a long time."

Luckily, they made the ferry on the hour and they boarded a mostly empty deck. They left the car to watch the shore slip away from the boat. The snow hung heavy and damp, unlike the prairie dry they were used to, and Megumi shuddered in her jacket. Her okā-san spread her arms out sideways and spun circles like she was in *The Sound of Music*. Megumi blushed, nervously looking at the other parked vehicles. But they were only locals, sleeping the twenty-minute ride like commuters on a subway. Only tourists got out of their cars. Hisako was trying to catch snowflakes on her tongue so Megumi trudged to the other side of the ferry and peered over the railing. The entire lake was covered in a thin skin of ice, the prow tearing through the white like it was a piece of canvas. Dark little cracks appeared on the surface and spread away across the expanse, zig-zagging fractures so far and fast away from the boat that Megumi's eyes couldn't follow.

"It's so quiet!" Hisako yelled over the throbbing roar of the engine.

"What?"

"It's so peaceful. Let me take your picture."

"Okā-san, this is boring. There's nothing here. It would make a boring picture."

"It's not for you, it's for me! Smile!"

Megumi showed teeth for her mother, then jerked her head toward the middle of the deck. "You'd better go to the washroom while you can. It's heated and there won't be another for a long time."

Her mother ran to the toilet, anxious about missing the disembarkation. Megumi shook her head and grinned.

Megumi had no idea where the turn-off for the correct logging road was and didn't want to show it. And so much snow! It was heavy and wet and in huge heaping drifts. The last time she was here, it was in the fall and now, under the canopy of white, everything looked different.

"Ummm, I think I'll turn around. We might have passed the road I'm looking for."

"I thought you said you knew where you're going!"

"I do! It's just hard to tell. I know I'll be able to recognize the road going back." Megumi smiled.

"We could go somewhere else. . . ."

"No! I promised you I'd take you to these hot springs. It's so beautiful. There's pine trees all around and the hot water bubbles from an overhang of rock. The snow is so cold and the water just steams so hot around you. It's almost like magic. And you feel so alive and fresh when you come out. Like everything is washed away. There's a public one close to here, but it's like a swimming pool. This natural one is special, I want you to feel it too."

"It sounds nice," Hisako said weakly.

Megumi drove for another twenty minutes before she found a place she could turn around. Then they drove back the way they came.

"There! I knew it! That's the road!"

"There's no road. That's just snow. And there's nowhere to park!"

"I brought a shovel!" Megumi beamed. She could almost smell the earthy sulfur bubbling from the rocks. Could hardly wait to sink into the steamy depths.

Megumi hopped out of the van and started furiously shovelling a space on the side of the road. Her okā-san peered out of the passenger window. Nibbling anxiously on pumpkin seeds. Megumi puffed, sweat trickling into her eyes, she shucked her toque and put her back into the shovel.

God! The snow was heavier than shit. But it wasn't going to stop her. She shovelled and pitched and heaved a spot just big enough to parallel park her car. Then gathered drinking water, towels, camera, and food, and stuffed it all in the backpack. Grinning the whole time. She pulled on a baseball cap and turned to her mom.

"Ready?"

Her okā-san looked tentatively up the snow-filled logging road. Up hill. There were old skidoo tracks and no sign of people.

"Yes," she said faintly. "How far did you say it was?"

"Oh, about a fifteen-minute walk!" Megumi waved like it would be a piece of cake.

"Let's go, then." Determined. Hisako pulled her toque down almost to her eyebrows and locked the car door.

Megumi walked in front. The snow was wet, so when she stepped, her foot sunk to about mid-shin, then stopped because of a crust of older snow beneath. Megumi tramped down the wet for her okā-san so she could follow more easily behind her.

"Isn't it beautiful!" Megumi gushed. Aspens mingled with the dark bark of the pines and firs, and their limbs were as green as bamboo. Big fat silent flakes of lacy snow drifted down. And the silence in the forest rang in their ears like glass bells.

"Huh, huh," her mother puffed. "Very pretty."

Megumi turned around to look at her. She could still see the car. Their footsteps stained the snow a turquoise blue.

"You're really out of shape. You need to get more exercise, you know," Megumi said encouragingly. She trudged on. "Beautiful," she exclaimed to herself. "Amazing –"

"Wah!"

It sounded like someone being punched in the chest.

Megumi spun around.

Her okā-san was face-first in the snow. Her one leg, plunged thigh-deep, had broken through the crust and the forward motion had pitched her down like a sack of rice. Her mother pushed her torso up and white clung to her face. Megumi snickered.

"Tasukete!" her mother wailed.

Megumi trudged back and grabbed her okā-san's hand and heaved. Brushed her off like she would her own children.

"Don't stomp so hard," Megumi scolded, then started walking up the hill again. "The crust won't hold if you stomp so – Wah!"

Megumi's face was cold wet in packed snow and not half as pretty as when it was falling in flakes from the sky. She could hear her mother laughing. She pushed herself up, amazed that the snow was that deep, her leg pushed down so far that her crotch rested on the surface.

"Help me up!"

"Shhhhh!" Hisako suspiciously panned her gaze across the forest. "Listen!"

"What!"

"Shuh!"

Silence.

Then, a light, slithering, hissing sound.

Megumi swung her head toward the source, saw a small stream of snow sliding off a bough and on to the logging road.

"It's our voices," Hisako whispered theatrically. "It's happened before. The sound of our voices is making the snow fall off the trees."

Silence.

"It's just coincidence!" Megumi said in a normal voice.

Sarasarasarasara.

"See! I told you!"

"Maybe so," Megumi agreed, crawling out of her leg trap, "but there's no need to whisper."

"That's how avalanches start! They start small and grow big like a tidal wave!"

"Okā-san, it's perfectly safe. Come on, we're wasting time."

The road dipped down, climbed, then swung up and around. Hisako huffed and puffed. Nervously watched snow trickling off the trees like they were dripping acid. Megumi noticed the numbered markers on the trees. Marker Two. Did they mark kilometres? Wasn't the hot spring around Marker Seven? Megumi bit her lip. She could hear her mother puffing like a small engine. And it didn't help that sometimes they broke through the snow and floundered like cattle. Megumi trudged faster and her mother, slower. When Megumi looked back, her okā-san was leaning against a tree, hand clasped to her chest.

"It's been longer than fifteen minutes. Huh, huh. You said it was a fifteen-minute walk to the springs! Huh, huh, huh. We've been walking for over half an hour!"

"Let's take a break!" Megumi yelled cheerfully. More snow slid off trees and hissed all around them. Hisako looked bitterly at her daughter and held a forefinger to her lips. Megumi waited for her mother to catch up, then gave her the water. Hisako gulped greedily until Megumi pulled the bottle away.

"You'll get a stomach ache."

"I've been thinking. We should have brought a chicken."

"What?"

"Well, the bears are asleep now."

"What are you talking about?"

"But there are mountain cats. They don't sleep."

"Lynx are shy. They don't like people."

"No!" Hisako hissed. "The big ones. The lions!"

"Oh. Cougars."

Hisako slowly looked all around, like uttering the word would invoke them.

"We should have brought a chicken. That way, we can throw them something while we're running away."

"Okā-san," Megumi sighed, "we're not going to be attacked by cougars."

"You have young children," Hisako muttered, almost to herself. "You can't die, but I guess my children are grown, it wouldn't be so bad. . . ."

"Shut up!" Megumi started trudging again. The snow falling a little heavier.

The road was straight for some time and Megumi stepped up her pace. Marker Four! After a while, she couldn't hear her okā-san's panting breath, so she turned around. Her mother was a good five hundred metres behind. Standing in the middle of the logging road. Both arms dangling. Megumi sighed. And walked back.

"Don't be mad," Hisako said. Her cheeks were flushed and her chest heaved up and down.

"It's just that we're not making good time." Megumi brushed off the snow that was piled on top of her okā-san's toque.

"Time! You said it was fifteen minutes from the car! We've been walking for over an hour!"

"Well if you wouldn't stop every ten steps you take!"

Snow hissed and slithered off trees.

"I'm not young, you know!" Hisako stated. "I'm almost sixty!"

"You're almost sixty?"

"Don't you know?"

"Ummm," Megumi bit her lip. Frowning. "I guess I hadn't really thought about it. I guess I just thought you were, well, Okā-san-aged. But sixty?"

"My heart is palpitating!"

"Don't exaggerate."

"It is. It's roaring in my ears. What if I have a heart attack?"

"You won't have a heart attack."

"You don't know where you're going, do you?" Hisako held both hands to her chest like an alien was going to burst out.

"I do! We're almost there. . . ."

"But you said fifteen minutes –"

"We walked in when there wasn't any snow," Megumi said weakly. And didn't add that she'd tried some 'shrooms that tasted quite healthy, and she was sure they hadn't worked at all. She hadn't felt particularly giddy or happy afterwards. Who knows, maybe it had altered time?

"We're almost there, I swear," Megumi encouraged. "You want a little chocolate for energy?"

"All right," Hisako sighed. Puffing slower and slower.

"I really want you to see those hot springs, Okā-san. They're really special and I want to share them with you."

Hisako patted chocolate-scented fingers against Megumi's rosy cheek.

When Hisako finished her snack, Megumi shouldered the backpack again.

"Why don't I walk ahead and scout out the road. You just take your time and I'll double back."

"You go," Hisako nodded. "I'll follow."

Megumi walked briskly, glancing up at the sky. The snow still fell, fat and smug and, somehow, not as pretty. But they were almost there! She knew it! And once they were in the water, the walk would be nothing. The warm sulfur breath of heat would melt the soreness from their muscles.

The road pitched into a steeper grade and Megumi's own breath wheezed in her chest. Guiltily, she looked around and her mother was a small figure trudging back-bent, like an old woman. What if she really did have a heart attack? Megumi didn't know real first aid. She thought she could build a travois with the towels and some saplings. At least she knew how they were made in theory. . . . She looped back down the steep road to her okā-san.

"I have to pee," her mother wheezed. Great puffs of breath clouding around her head. The temperature was dropping.

"Just pee here," Megumi pointed.

"Here?"

"No one's coming!" Megumi exclaimed.

"But here. Plain as day. In the middle of a forest on a logging road. . . ." Hisako said unhappily. Blinking.

"Animals pee here all the time!"

Her okā-san's lower lip trembled.

"Oh, for god's sake!" Megumi lowered the backpack and got out one of the bath towels. Held up the two corners to make a screen.

When Hisako was done, she furiously kicked snow over the telltale yellow hole that melted deep into the drift.

"No one's going to know that it was a person," Megumi pointed out.

"I'll know," Hisako determinedly kicked some more.

Megumi sighed. The sun was much lower. And the sky had a light mauve cast. "Let's eat our lunch," she said. Eyeing Marker Six that glowed tantalizingly from a tree.

Hisako led Megumi a good distance away from the yellow snow. Megumi took out two plastic shopping bags for them to sit on, and opened their lunch of onigiris and sweet egg omelet. They didn't talk. Just ate. Megumi realizing how bone-tired she was herself, when the food settled into her stomach. She fished her mother's camera out of the pack and stood back to take a picture. Her okā-san's cheeks were flushed bright red and her eyes drooped with exhaustion. Hisako smiled weakly, bravely holding up the water bottle for a pose. Snap. Shot of an almost sixty-year-old mother before collapsing from a heart attack. Young woman forces mother on winter hike, walks her to exhaustion. This and more on tonight's news at ten. Megumi sighed. Glanced once more at Marker Six, then put away the camera.

"Should we turn back after lunch?" she offered.

Hisako looked up from her snow picnic hesitantly. "I know how badly you want to go to the hot springs."

"I don't want to go so badly I'll force you when it's making you feel awful."

"Really?"

"It's a holiday, right?"

"You won't be mad at me later?"

"What do you take me for?" Megumi asked.

"I felt like I was a child, being dragged along behind a mean mother. I even had tears in my eyes."

"Oh! I'm sorry. I didn't know you felt that bad. We can drive down to the public one. It's not as nice, but it'll be warm."

"We've been walking for over three hours," Hisako looked at her watch. "It's getting kind of dark, don't you think, ha-ha."

"It'll be faster going downhill," Megumi promised.

It *was* faster going downhill, but it still took over an hour. Almost full dark by the time they were in the car, Hisako was sniffing and Megumi didn't know if it was only her nose, or if she was crying. The snow fell faster and heavier and the road was a white blur. It wound and turned such lakeside curves that Megumi's mother scrabbled in her handbag for Kleenex to wring.

Finally, there was a faint glow of light among the screen of trees. Megumi sighed with relief. The parking lot was empty. The orange light was an eerie circle of bright in the falling snow. Hisako, too weary to talk, followed her daughter into the wooden building. They rented coarse baggy swimsuits from a bored young man and changed in a room that smelled of chlorine and wet cedar. Hisako sat slouched on a bench, too exhausted to be worried about catching communicable diseases from the public wood.

"Megumi-chan?"

"Hai?"

"Why did you and Barney part ways?"

Megumi gulped, ducked her head to pull on her swimming suit. Turned her back to stuff her clothes into a locker. "I was lonely," she said slowly. Slipped the token into the slot and listened to it drop. "I was really lonely for a long time." Megumi briskly turned around. "Shall we go?"

The cold outside was a gasp against their skin, but the pool. . . . The dark night circled the bubble of light around the pool, and the water, lit from beneath, was a translucent blue green. The snow fell in huge wet flakes, straight up and down in the windless sky. Megumi could almost hear the hiss of ice crystals melting in the glowing water. She looked across to her okā-san, and they smiled at each other.

"Oh," they sighed, when they stepped inside. Ankles, calves, wet warmth curling up their knees and across their thighs. The liquid heat seeped into muscles, bone, and they lay back to float as if in outer space. Heat all around, only the surface chill of snow melting on their faces, their palms. Megumi reached out to hold her mother's hand. Fingers clasped, they gazed upward, the snow falling down looked like stars flying past.

Home Stay

"I've got single portions of ground beef all froze up in the freezer. That standing one, not the lying down one," Gloria yelled into the phone, across endless prairie miles, endless winter-dried coulees, sorry stretches of willow shrub and, miraculously, into Jun's ear. "We should be back by eleven the latest and you can fry up ground beef even if it's froze through. There's spaghetti sauce in the pantry."

Jun pulled the receiver five centimetres away from his head. Nodded in reply.

"Just keep on stirring is all," Gloria shouted.

"Don't burn down the house, ha, ha," Karl bellowed from the background.

"Oh dear," Jun heard Gloria murmuring to her husband as she set down the receiver, "he might not −" Click.

Jun shivered, shuddered, his palms burning with ice, but he could not drop what he held in his hands. His stomach writhed like a salt-sprinkled slug and he could actually feel beads of sweat sliding down the bones of his spine.

The stuff he had casually unwrapped, the stuff he had found in the upright deep freeze with its old-fashioned press lock. The stuff was not ground beef.

Five bulbous goldfish.

They were swollen fatter than bursting, eyes protruding gelatinous, each tattered fin, every glittering scale gleaming in a thin casing of ice. Mouths gaped forever.

Salt pooled tidal in the deep of Jun's mouth and he ran to the washroom, hands held out in front of him. Spine convulsing, his stomach milking bile, Jun didn't drop the fish, just ran, cradling the very thing that revolted. But he made it, some strange sensibility made him toss the goldfish into the toilet, and he bent his back to heave dryly into the sink.

Janine had called his back poetic. Said she could never imagine loving anyone with chest hair now that she'd been with him. Janine said a lot of things and meant them. At the time. But she had left him for good when he brought her *Baywatch* beach sandals as a souvenir from San Diego.

"How could you?" she'd uttered coldly.

"What do you mean?"

"Do you know what kind of program *Baywatch* is?"

"Well, it's about lifeguards, I think. Does it matter?"

"Jun," Janine sank down to the floor.

Jun blinked rapidly. Janine was so, well, strong. Never show weakness or be damned. He squatted down, peered at her face while he blinked and blinked. She swung away from his gaze.

"I'm sorry?" Jun started.

"Jun," Janine pinched her lips until they disappeared inside her mouth. She caught his hands. Clenched. Let them go. "It's not going to work out. I'm sorry. I thought I might get used to it, but I can't."

"What?"

Love is never enough.

They had been married thirteen months.

Jun never did figure out exactly what "it" was. He could only begin
at the sandals and trace a vague route backwards. The sandals, the
Japanese condoms, the butternut squash, the recliner. . . . Gloria and
Karl had been horrified. And guilt-ridden.

"It's because we spoiled her something awful, she came to us
when we were almost forty," Karl apologized. Bobbing his bearish
head.

"She's not a bad girl," Gloria dripped tears. "She just gets set in
her ways and nothing can change her mind."

"You're a good son-in-law, Jun. I wasn't none too pleased when
we first met, to be honest," Karl confessed, ignoring Gloria's tiny
jerk of chin. "I don't hold much on folks marrying people from different countries, hard enough when you're marrying your own. But
you're a decent man. Kind. Generous. Janine could have done a lot
worse. She probably will," Karl said. Picked at a blackened thumbnail that was starting to come off.

"You move on in with us," Gloria offered. "Until you get your
bearings. It's the least we can do."

"We need a young guy to look after our livestock!" Karl winked.

Janine had wanted to keep the pizza shop they ran together. Jun
didn't care much for pizza or the business, so Janine bought him out,
kept their old apartment, and Jun moved in with her parents.

Jun quite liked the chores, the repetitive nature of caring for animals. The sensible dailiness about it was comforting and he slipped
into the pattern with satisfaction if not pleasure. The dawn walk-
about to look for early dropped calves. Hauling hay and feed to the
wintering pasture. Milking the dreamy-eyed Jersey, old-fashioned

style. The frantic flurry of chickens, Guinea hens, the wonder of their blue eggs. Slops and hash for the tragic pigs. Jun wished there were horses so he could write postcards to his college friends: "Married a white girl, got divorced. Now I'm a cowboy." Just as well, Jun thought. He'd started noticing that things he'd thought were matter of fact, concrete, weren't necessarily so. A wife. A home. What was solid could turn liquid. It confused him and made him terribly absent-minded. Probably break his neck if he was on a horse.

Jun dabbed toilet paper to the seam of his lips. He ran the faucet even though there was nothing to wash away, concerned that there might be an invisible film of odour on the surface of the sink and Gloria might wonder.

Goldfish! Dead goldfish! What were they doing in the freezer? Jun shuddered and he clenched his teeth to bite back the salt that rose once more. He couldn't bear to look at them, now golden blobs bobbing in the toilet bowl. Four hours until Gloria and Karl got home. He'd decide what to do with them after he'd settled his stomach, might help if he ate something. Tomato sauce was out of the question.

The freezer door was still open, cold misting the kitchen. Jun hurried to press it shut and tried not to imagine what else might be frozen inside. A well-loved cat that Gloria and Karl had euthanized? A treasured parakeet? Still-born puppies? Jun shuddered, wrapped icy arms around his middle. Who could have done this thing? Practical Gloria? Tell-it-like-it-is Karl? What kind of person saved dead goldfish in a deep freeze?

Jun boiled spaghetti, but didn't bother with a sauce, just fried the noodles with a good dab of home-made butter, fresh garlic, salt, and parmesan cheese. He liked Gloria's kitchen. She had the habit of keeping a kettle on low boil on the gas stove. For moisture, she said and Jun had taken to the habit too. The thin wet whine was almost companionable. He ate his simple dinner and drank iron-tasting water that came out of Gloria and Karl's well.

"Don't go," his mother had said, looking at the clock that hung above the doorway. The always-on television blared behind his back.

Jun hadn't answered. Blinked. Blinked. Had stared at the hot water pot, plastic decal of a tiger, peeling and brown-curled. It was so old. He should have got her a new one.

"You're the only one now." His okā-san tapped tea leaves into the red-clay tea pot. She palmed the press on the hot water urn, hiss of liquid boiled, spouting. His mother poured tea with her diamond-shaped hands, nudged a cup into his palms. They drank. Jun, sip, sipping. The always-on television, pots dangling on hooks above the sink tinked through the dull roar of a semi-trailer on the raised freeway, Kubota's, next door, laughing over a late dinner, the noodle soup seller playing his plaintive tune, a beacon for the last hungry business men straggling off a late subway. Jun sipped and sipped loudly until his cup was empty, until his mother reached out her hand. She poured more tea for him. They drank, filling the pot from the electric urn, nudging cups back and forth until all of the water was gone.

"Well," his okā-san wrapped up sweet bean manju for him to take back to college. "I guess it's time."

Jun ducked his head and slipped his light jacket over his graceful back. The air was sweet with fall and the metal stairs click-clacked under his shoes. When he looked up, his mother was not watching from the kitchen window.

His mother never cooked with butter, but that was something he'd taken to as well, since living with Gloria and Karl. Janine wouldn't touch the stuff, called it teat grease. Cooked butter always tasted good, but Jun hated the way the stuff congealed after it cooled down. Traces left on his plate squirming with the pattern of pasta, weals of hardening grease like sand-worm tracks left on the beach. And how awful, the water. When Janine had first taken Jun to visit her parents and he tasted their well water, he had spewed it back out into the sink. Gloria and Karl had laughed.

"It's because there's so much iron and the water's so hard," Karl had gasped. Wiping his eyes. "You'll get used to it. And you can't even tell when you make up some coffee."

Later on in the day, Jun had poured the kettle for tea and was shocked when chunks of white rock fell out. He had thought they were playing a trick on him, hard water, ha, ha. And when he told them this, they burst out laughing until they cried, Janine rolling on the linoleum, then running to the washroom, bladder held by desperate hands.

"Come in," his mother had said, a small dimple in her cheek though she wasn't smiling. His okā-san in the steamy pool of the public bath and the water cupped her neck. Jun had taken small, careful steps on slippery tiles. Had placed one foot in the hot liquid.

"Ohhhh," he mouthed. One step. Then another. The silky water sliding up his thin and childish legs, his still baby-blue bum. The public bath echoed with the voices of other small children, laughing with mothers, grandmothers, aunties. But the steam softened the sounds cloudy. The other patrons were misty shapes, not solid.

"Lie back," his mother murmured. And Jun had. The soft silk heat of liquid surrounding. His mother held him, floating, with only one diamond-shaped hand gently cupping the back of his neck.

Jun smiled. Stopped smiling with a sudden flurry of blinks.

The goldfish. Still in the toilet. Shit. But he didn't feel squeamish any more. Funny, he thought. Why had he in the first place? He put the frying pan, plate, cutlery into the sink, and poured perpetually boiling water on top of everything. Watched the reams of used butter melt away. Jun ignored the washroom and went in to watch television.

He never sat in Karl's recliner, some sort of territorial reflex, he wasn't sure, but Karl had etched his body into the leather, and sitting in it would be like sitting in his lap.

"Let's fuck here," Janine had giggled. Gloria and Karl long gone to bed, still chuckling about hard water.

"What?"

"I want to fuck in Karl's chair!" Janine pushed Jun backward so he thumped heavily into the Karl-shaped leather, Janine tugging her sweater over her head as she giggled. Jun withered in his underpants. Janine stuck her tongue between Jun's slender lips, curved her hands down the graceful lines of his back. When Janine slipped her hand inside Jun's waistband, he felt innocuous. An exposed salamander.

"Isn't that just like a man!" Janine had thrown her exaggerated hands into the air and stomped to the basement. Left Jun in the cradle of Karl's lap.

No, Jun sat now, neatly on the beige Sears sofa, feet placed on the shag carpet.

Gloria and Karl didn't have satellite and sitcoms held no humour for Jun. He'd heard that that was the last test of whether or not you've mastered another language. If you could understand humour. Jun blinked and blinked. He stared at the television, the roars of recorded laughter, until Gloria's ridiculous cuckoo clock ground out a sound. 10:30. Gloria and Karl. Shit. Jun's lips curled toward his right cheekbone, a Janine-imitation he had picked up. He hoped that any deep emotional ties Gloria and Karl may have had with the dead goldfish were well frozen. How bonded could a person get to fish anyway? He knew some people in Japan sat in their koi ponds and fed the glorious creatures from their hands. Koi, he could understand, but really, who in their right mind would have *feelings* for these mutated excuses of pets?

Chopsticks would be just the thing to get them out of the toilet with ease, but Karl "would starve to death if they ever had to eat with sticks," so Gloria had none in the house. Jun would have to ladle the carcasses out.

He found a slotted spoon in the third drawer beside the stove, a Ziploc bag in the pantry. He would put those disgusting creatures back in the freezer and next time someone went looking for single portions of ground beef, they'd damn well see what it wasn't before they'd unwrapped it.

Jun nudged the washroom door with his foot. Flicked the light switch on with his elbow. Swallowed. Blinked.

The deformed fish.

Those coffins of ice. Melted.

And alive.

The tattered fish, the undead fish, swam in sluggish circles in the iron-stained stink of the toilet bowl. Gills gaping, broken fins ragged with remnants of disease. Their popped-o mouths, open, shutting, thawing from an icy sleep into an awakening hunger. The tiny hairs on Jun's arms, nape, the curve of his graceful back, rose and tingled cold crazy. Shuddered almost into wet.

My god. My god. A miracle. A sick sick miracle. A portent. A fucking sign. He made a small noise. Ladle clattering to the floor.

"What – Jun? Are you okay?" Gloria knocked at the partially open bathroom door. She was pushed in by Karl, crowding, concerned. Together, they peered at Jun, caught movement in the toilet bowl, pressed forward to stare into the toilet. Gloria and Karl, their eyes popped, bulged in disbelief, mouths O in wonder and Jun guf-fawed, couldn't hold it back, gasped hysterical from the pit of his belly. He bellowed, one hand holding his gut and the other pointing to the miracle of the fishes, pointing back to Gloria and Karl. He convulsed with laughter, unable to stop, barely able to stand.

Gloria pinched her lips inside her mouth.

Karl flushed the toilet.

Jun's body contorted, gasping, tears streaming down his face, choking laughter like vomit. It's not funny! he thought. There's nothing funny, only to be torn apart with an explosive guffaw. Gloria lowered the lid of the bowl and determinedly sat Jun down. He gulped air, erupting with convulsive gasps, swallowing it into his slender body. Trembling with the effort. Gloria reached out both arms and pulled Jun's face into her soft bosom.

She smelled like baby powder.

Jun blinked. Blinked.

Jun wondered if he ought to move his head side to side between the cushy orbs of Gloria's breast.

Jun wondered if this was a motherly gesture on Gloria's part or if he was supposed to get physically excited. Perhaps both at the same time, in that Occidental way?

Jun wondered what good ol' Karl was thinking.

He pulled his head slightly back and tipped his eyes upwards. Karl loomed over Gloria's shoulder. A grin on his bearish face, he gave Jun a thumbs-up sign. Jun shook his head slightly.

"There, there," Gloria murmured, stroking Jun's glossy hair with one hand, keeping his head in her bosom with the other. "There, there."

What should he do? Jun wondered. What did they mean? Something felt terribly off, but he couldn't put words to it, it only yawned before him in growing darkness and he scrambled away from the crumbling edge. The goldfish, Jun thought, just think about the goldfish.

"Goldfish," he muttered.

"Shhhh, shhhhhhh," Gloria murmured. "They're gone now, don't worry your head about it." She gestured her chin toward Jun and Karl knelt down in front of him. Karl slipped one arm under the back of Jun's knees and behind his back with the other. Karl lifted Jun up like he were an injured animal, a well-loved pet, and Jun's eyes gasped open.

A grown man! Carried like this! Jun could feel the verge, the tip of the chasm and he shuddered, shuddered at the incredible depths, the vertigo plunge and – and –

"He must be freezing!" Karl exclaimed.

"It's the shock," Gloria said decisively. "Let's put him in our room. We can turn up the heat on the waterbed."

Gloria pulled back the satiny covers and Karl deposited Jun on the unstable surface. It sloshed beneath him like nausea. The sheets smelled of Gloria's baby powder, Karl's hand cream, and Jun's teeth chattered though he hadn't thought he was cold. Karl leaned over him to unbutton his shirt, Gloria tugging the socks off his feet.

Someone started tugging on the fly of his jeans.

"Yamete," Jun whispered, clutching at his pants.

"Leave him be," he heard Gloria advise, her voice low. "He can sleep with his jeans on for one night, at least. Poor pet. He can sleep between us and we'll keep him warm."

"He's shivering away!" Karl exclaimed. "You've got to fatten him up some, Glory, he's all skin and bones. He's lighter than you are!"

"Oh, you stop!" Gloria giggled. Tucking the satiny comforter firmly around Jun's slender neck.

"Do you think, ah," Karl coughed, "the child's been a bit touched?"

"Oh, honey, I just don't know." Gloria smoothed the hair from Jun's brow and he stared upward. Not blinking. "We can't really know what he's thinking, can we?"

"He's like a son to me, a real son," Karl stated.

"He's as pretty as a cat," Gloria murmured. She changed into her flannel nightdress and sloshed into bed. Sat up, absentmindedly stroking Jun's glossy hair, watched Karl put on his pyjamas.

"Leave the hall light on. In case he gets worse during the night," Gloria called out. So Karl just switched off the bedroom light, the weight of the door slowly swinging itself shut. And as Karl sloshed into the bed on the other side of Jun, their middle-aged backs fencing him in between them, the door slowly closed, and the wedge of light slivered into darkness.

From Across
a River

She is three. Breathless. Fever presses her forehead like a hot and heavy hand. Her father sits on the edge of her bed, a silver razor blade pinched between his thumb and forefinger.

"The blood is sick," he explains gently as he clasps her wrist in a soft but firm grip. He slices the tender flesh, a parting of meat and sinew, white, red, and gleaming.

Emiko just watches, her lips slightly dry. There is no pain. Only wonder that her father is capable of doing this.

"We have to let the bad blood out."

She wants to ask why, but words don't leave her lips. The gap between thought and action is so wide a decade will pass before he ever hears her. But her father shakes his head. Frowns. He murmurs something with excruciating slowness, the sound ballooning round and full. It will surely pop.

Kelsey, who was sleeping beside her, jerked erect. "Don't I have school this morning?" her childish voice shattering the ether of sleep.

Emiko started, heart thudding and swollen. Mouth gasping for air. She jerked upright and slapped for the alarm clock. A half-hearted *ting*. She stared at the hands in the winter darkness: 7:25.

"Oh!" Emiko flapped bedding off her sock-covered feet and pulled on the sweatsuit she'd left on the floor. She ran for her daughter's clothing in the bathroom, then rushed back. The child had burrowed deep beneath the blankets. Emiko flipped on the lights. "Four and a half more minutes until the bus," she sang.

"I'm cold," Kelsey whined, her voice muffled beneath three layers. "It's still dark outside."

Emiko pulled the covers off.

"You're mean! The lights! Turn off the lights!"

"You're going to miss the bus!" Emiko grinned through her teeth. She started to stuff a sock on her daughter's foot, forcing the bunched-up wool over resisting toes.

Kelsey screamed. The child's maw unhinged a wail that filled the small bedroom, spilling into the hallway, and Emiko, heart stopping, dropped the girl's small ankle. Her fingers crept to cover her horrified lips.

No. She hadn't hurt the child.

Scrabbling, Emiko clutched her daughter's limb, poring over the long fine bones, so unlike her own. Was that a bruise? No. Only a vein close to the smooth surface: blue and filled with life.

Emiko sat down. Shoulders sagging her back into its familiar curl. 7:28. Was it possible?

No.

Something shuffling at the doorway.

"Daddy!" Kelsey held up thin arms. Gordon bent down to sweep her into his strong hold. Curly hairs glinted auburn. Kelsey latched on to his waist with her legs and clasped her childish arms around his neck. She turned to glare down at her mother. No longer bawling, but a few fat tears still clung to the corners of the child's lashes.

"Mommy's mean! She hurt my toe!"

Emiko slowly raised her head. She could see up Gordon's nose and a clot of hanakuso stuck to several nostril hairs. It fluttered with his breathing.

"Why don't I get you ready for school, pumpkin? Then we can drive there together, just you and me!"

"I love you, Daddy!"

Gordon turned, carrying his daughter to her own room. The child rested her chin on her father's shoulder and smiled at her mother. Emiko watched her daughter's face with a measure of distaste. Kelsey smiled even broader, her canines too pointed to be cute, her dark eyes gleaming brightly, like a fox. Emiko started, blinked, but the child closed her eyes. Emiko shook her head. Kelsey's clothing on the bed. No point in dressing her in a whole new set when these were still perfectly fine.

"Ta –" Emiko choked, gulped at the stale morning air. The word a spasm in her mouth, she swallowed hard. Blood in her ears drumming loud. Fast. Her armpits pressed moistly against her sides and a fine coating of sweat chilled her entire back. Shivering, Emiko crawled back into her blankets. The light was still on, but she could pull the pillow over her head. Emiko could barely hear Kelsey's excited chatter about getting pancakes instead of cold cereal.

When she woke up, there was a sourness in her mouth. Emiko swallowed. She felt slightly sweaty, surprised that she had actually fallen asleep. She hadn't slept properly for over a month, and the days and nights waxed and waned with a fevered conflation of forgetfulness and hyper-reality.

Emiko hated the wooden chair at her desk. She tried to keep

clothing draped over the back, but the sweater she had left the night before had fallen to the floor. Emiko flicked her eyes away from the mesmerizing grain of wood. Faux patterns, she told herself. Not even real wood. Her eyes, unwittingly, slid back. The markings swirled clockwise, counter-clockwise, a twisting twining of cells and time. And as she gazed, the wood undulated, liquid lines morphing into shape, eyes, mouths. Howling. Wailing oni writhed from the swirl of wood, spiral demonic horns twirling upward, malformed cats crawling out of the grain.

She started. A sound almost breaching her lips.

The chair was just a chair.

Emiko blinked rapidly, dragging the back of her hand over her closed eyes. The overloud ticking of the clock. She glanced up. 10:37.

She didn't want to pick up the child at the bus stop.

Emiko creaked down the long hallway into the kitchen, the refrigerator clunking into operation, whining on the borderline between sound and words.

The clutter of breakfast dishes was left unwashed on the kitchen table and counters. Drying eggshells, syrup spilled, and an almost-full two-litre carton of milk turning thick and sour. A platter of cold pancakes. No one ever ate cold pancakes. Emiko sighed. Her stomach gurgled. She pinched a piece from the stack, brought the morsel to her lips. The slightly greasy smell wafted into her nose. Her mouth pooled with a salty liquid. Emiko dropped the piece back on the plate, brushing her hands against sweatpants. Little lumps along her thigh; she glanced down. A row of transparent dried grains of rice stuck to the cloth and she absentmindedly picked them off with her fingernail. Dropped them on the floor.

Seven wasted pancakes! Who did he think would eat them all? Emiko sliced the stack of soggy circles into bits with sticky cutlery, crumbs spilling from the edge of the platter. There was a small blur of movement. A thudding of motion or sound. Something thrown at her head. Emiko ducked, arms encircling her skull, her heart pounding. Then she looked up.

No. Just a glimpse of someone's back passing through the frame of her kitchen window, walking past her house in the back alley. Emiko shook her head. Dragged both palms over her face and pressed down on her closed eyelids with her fingertips. The pressure left an afterimage of green lights. She wished that the slats on the back fence weren't so widely spaced. They didn't live in a bad neighbourhood, but who knew what could happen in a back alley? There was no security.

Emiko glared down the hallway to the closed door facing her. The floorboards weren't flat and the doorways were slightly skewed. She thought she could hear soft breathing from Gordon's room. He must be sleeping again. Or lying in bed, staring at the ceiling. There was a time when Emiko had loved the fact that her husband worked at home.

Emiko snatched a piece of paper and scrawled, "You pick up Kelsey at the bus stop." She crept down the long hall to crouch at her husband's closed door. She slid the piece of paper across the floorboards.

"What are you doing?" Gordon loomed.

Emiko fell backward on to her plump behind.

She pushed back her heavy bangs. Emiko stared up at her husband from the hardwood floor. He was so tall that his head looked like it was shrunken at the top of his skinny neck. The hanakuso still fluttered in his left nostril.

"You have snot in your nose," Emiko stated.

A bright pink crept up Gordon's pale neck and on to his unshaven cheeks. He anxiously pinched both nostrils with thumb and forefinger, once, twice, as he inhaled, managing to plaster the clump along the inner lining. Emiko was relieved. As long as she didn't have to watch it flap.

"You're not talking to me," Gordon said, in his reasonable voice. "We need to talk."

Emiko stood and brushed off her bottom. She handed Gordon the note and went back into the kitchen.

"Kelsey really needs you right now!" Gordon shook the message in the air. Emiko turned her back, the plate of pancakes heavy in her hands.

"We need to be a family more than ever," Gordon pleaded as his wife plodded three steps down to the second landing.

"What kind of mother are you?" he muttered. His head sagging on his bony neck.

Emiko stuffed her broad feet into Gordon's winter boots. She had to turn her toes upward with each step to keep them on, but at least they were too big to bump up against her bunions.

What kind of mother was she?

She hadn't bothered with a coat though hummocks of old snow still lay on the ground. The chinook-warm winds mimicked spring again. The scent of mud rose from the thawing lawn. Bile rose in Emiko's throat. Choking, she swallowed the bitter acid back down. She clumped to the picnic table in their backyard.

"Scrawwwk! Scrawwwwk!" she shrieked. Scattering handfuls of pancake.

"You feeding those damn scavengers again?"

Emiko twitched and turned around.

"You keep your magpies away from my chickadees!" Hal teased. Emiko's neighbour rested his jowly chin on the adjoining fence. His plump hands gripped the wood and they looked like white mitts beside his face

Emiko bent her lips upward.

"You noticed the house three doors down was bought? Haven't seen the new neighbours, though. You?"

Emiko shook her head.

Hal lowered his friendly voice. "You folks need to get out more. Alone time, just you and ol' Gord. Me and the missus'll be happy to watch Kelsey for you. She's a little angel!"

Emiko managed to control a shiver, her broken smile flattening into something else. She nodded and turned to flip the last of the pancake off the plate.

"I'm serious about the offer," Hal called to her back.

Emiko clumped back into the house and slipped out of Gordon's galoshes. She sat on the steps and squeezed her feet into her own leather boots. They pressed painfully against the triangles of bone jutting out from the joints beneath her big toes. Bunions ran in her family. She hoped Kelsey didn't get them when she grew older. Pulled on her jacket and slipped outside.

It was quite a jaunt to the supermarket, especially with her bunioned feet. But Emiko would never drive again. And the last thing she needed was to be stuck with Gordon in the confines of the car. His kind voice and sane patience were more than she could endure.

They needed new milk. Some more fruit. Cold cuts.

Warm wind is an unnatural thing in the middle of winter, Emiko thought. She still couldn't get used to the erratic temperatures despite eight years of it. She minced down the brown slush of the back alley. The treads of her boots were more fashionable than practical and they shot out at any given moment. Her bunions ached. She watched her feet, toeing the patches that had more gravel. The telephone wires guided her periphery. The banks of snow along

the sides of the alley were big enough to cover dead bodies, but
she didn't want to look in case they were. Magpies clamoured from
someone's yard and Emiko quickly glanced upward. Certainly they
harboured her no ill will. In other countries, birds ate from the dead.
But Emiko made sure the birds that visited her yard only partook
of what the living had eaten. They were not harbingers of woe. And
cats, unlucky or not, were scarce after the recent by-law. Emiko tee-
tered on uneven gravel, the stickiness of mud.

A waft of mould, incense. She practically smacked into the
stranger's back.

"Oh!" Emiko clucked. She glanced up. Who could possibly be
walking more slowly than she was?

The figure was bundled overly-warm for chinook weather. An
industrial work coat with a fake wool collar was pulled high around
the neck and chin. The person trudged, back slightly bent, hands
crammed into deep pockets. A red-brown toque over coarse grey
hair. Walking stiffly, with slightly bowed legs, crab-like, her steps
were quick and jerky. Oddly, she didn't seem to cover much ground.

Her, Emiko thought, though nothing would give any clue to
the person's sex. The clothes looked mannish, but the bow-legged
steps reminded Emiko of her aging mother. Must be an immigrant,
Emiko thought, uttering a small cough so that the stranger wouldn't
be startled by her coming up from behind. Emiko quickened her
steps. The brown slush splashed up on her sweatpants, but she was
curious to see the stranger's face. She must be the new neighbour.
Arms swinging brisk and straight, Emiko trotted with pinched feet.
Turning her head slightly to her left, she strained toward the stranger's shoulder. Trying to get a good look. She stepped faster, craning,
breath coming in little puffs. How could she stand to be bundled
like that, Emiko wondered. She must be from a hot country.

Emiko's right foot shot out forty-five degrees, her left knee gave out, and she shrieked, landing smack in icy slush, her bottom simultaneously soaked and bruised. Mouth flapping up and down, she was uncertain if she ought to laugh or cry. How embarrassing! Falling just like that, like a middle-aged person. Emiko shook her head for the stranger's benefit, then raised her eyes to look for a hand extended in aid.

But none was offered.

Emiko quickly looked over her shoulder. The hunched-up jacket was scuttling away, going back where she came from, hands still plunged in pockets.

"Oh!" Hot tears burned inside Emiko's eyelids. She held her forearm over her eyes and had a bit of a cry until her wet behind prickled numb and itchy. Emiko stiffly pushed herself up, bottom raised like a toddling child. She was soaked through and her clothes a mess. Well, she thought. Well, it was time to wash her sweatpants anyway. When she was upright, the heel of her right boot flapped uselessly and she almost turned her ankle. Emiko's lower lip wobbled. Pressed her forearm over her eyes then shook her head with determination. She would go home. Bathe. Eat a little lunch.

Kelsey looked up from a plate of bright orange macaroni and cheese. Her childish mouth turned down and her nose wrinkled.

"You're a mess!" she scolded. "Isn't Mommy a mess, Daddy?" Kelsey beamed at her father.

Gordon clumsily stood up. The chair fell backward as he rushed to Emiko, his hands outstretched. His pale face bloodless.

"What happened? Are you okay? Did someone –"

Emiko jerked her arms out of Gordon's grip and stepped away from his concern. She plunked down on the top stair and tugged clenching boots off swollen feet.

"I just slipped," she muttered. When she stood, there was a brown heart-shaped smear on the pale green linoleum.

"Look!" Kelsey giggled. "Mom pooped her pants!"

Blood pumped upward into Emiko's head though she couldn't say, later, exactly why. But the boot with the flappy heel was in her hand and she threw it at the back door, fracturing the glass, cracks zigzagging outward in a pretty pattern.

There was a denseness in the air, forcing Emiko to pant. She turned to look at the people in her kitchen.

The child gulped, sobbed. The orange of macaroni inside her mouth.

Gordon ran to his daughter and scooped her up in his strong arms, shushing, murmuring into her auburn hair. His eyes burned Emiko's face with something she'd never seen before.

How curious, Emiko thought, as she descended the stairs to the laundry room.

"We're going away for a little while," Gordon called to her back in his reasonable voice. "I'm taking Kelsey and we'll stay at my mom's. You call us when you want to talk."

Emiko gave a little wave without looking back, but Gordon had already carried Kelsey to her bedroom.

The basement was cold and a metallic stench hung in the air. Emiko looked quickly over her shoulder. The hot water tank squatted on the concrete. Small balls of dust and hair moved ever so slightly in the currents of air. The doorway to the adjoining room was closed. What was behind it? Nothing. Just silliness.

Emiko, teeth clacking, peeled wet clothing off her body, shoving everything in the washer. Naked, she looked down at her jiggling belly, the inverted pucker of her scar. She fingered the old pink weal with her forefinger. Kelsey had come into this world, bawling, headfirst. But Ta – but the other had to be cut out. She shuddered, shook, arms clamped her soft middle. Her gut heaved and a thin stream of yellow shot from her mouth. The acid burn of bile in the back of her throat. She stared at the yellow splatter on the concrete. Emiko shuffled to the filthy basement shower, arms still holding her stomach as though she carried something precious.

The blast of hot water soon filled the small bathroom and Emiko stood beneath the spray, mouth open. The water tasted sweet and she swallowed though she knew that there were unhealthy things in the hot water tank. Eyes closed. The pounding of the spray pierced like needles and tore into her flesh, flesh that softened, ripped open rotten and stinking. Emiko shut the knobs and flung open the smelly curtain. The small room was filled with steam and the after-roar of the water rang in her ears, like the voices of people calling from across a river.

There was no towel hanging on the rack. Emiko walked upstairs, leaving wet puddles on the steps. Kelsey and Gordon were gone. The kitchen, Emiko noted, was still a mess. Lunch and breakfast dishes, both, but she was heated down to the marrow and for this she was grateful. Movement. Just beyond her periphery. She ducked, as if dodging a rock thrown. She scrabbled around, forearm holding in her sagging breasts, but it was only someone walking through the frame of her kitchen window. Emiko scuttled to peer out the glass. The back of an industrial overcoat. Bow-legged crab-walk. *Her* again! Emiko was certain that it must be the new neighbour Hal had mentioned. Horrible, horrible person!

Emiko stared until the stranger's back was obstructed by Hal's fence.

Why hadn't the stranger helped her? In fact, the woman must have pushed her down! She had been attacked! The world was a terrible and dangerous place. Emiko shivered, her belly and bottom jiggling, and she ran, crouched, to her bedroom.

Emiko crawled into her nest of blankets. Unwashed sheets smelling slightly sweet with an animal musk. Emiko curled up and closed her eyes. Her stomach squeezed on itself, a gurgling protest, and she clasped both arms over her soft belly. Her tongue tasted sour inside the hole of her mouth. No food could possibly pass there. Her stomach rumbled. Perhaps she could eat her tongue, feed herself with her own body and eliminate the element that tasted bad in the first place.

Emiko's eyes burned grainy dry.

There was a stillness outside that sounded of falling snow.

If only on that day.

If only, that day, she had sat at the kitchen table for a few seconds longer.

If only she had gone to sleep a few moments earlier the night before.

What would have happened if she'd spent more time on her hair?

If she had made pancakes instead of toast, the entire day would have been different, a few minutes changing the course of the future by taking a bath instead of a shower or making the classroom treat in the morning instead of the evening before or talking on the phone with her mother for longer than she'd planned or deciding to wear a shirt with buttons instead of a pullover sweater, she'd be living five seconds later and it would have changed the course of her life only she'd – that day would –

If she'd never left Japan none of this would have come to be. Did every action in her life come to this place?

What if –
What if it had been Kelsey instead. . . .

What kind of mother was she?

It was with a weary surprise that Emiko woke. Her head thick with unrestful sleep, a cry slipped out of her mouth just as her eyes opened and she wondered at the noise. Did she sound like that?

The street lamps shone a cool orange through the curtains and the red light flashed from her answering machine. How had she slept through the ringing? Emiko pursed her lips. Whatever the message, she didn't want to hear it. What she needed was a cup of tea. Emiko pulled on a T-shirt and corduroy pants. Woollen socks. She didn't look at the back of her wooden chair. Left her room, ripe with the smell of old sweat. A whisper of sound down the length of the hallway. The floorboards creaking beneath her weight.

The moonlit night cast odd shadows in the kitchen and Emiko avoided looking at the humped shoulders of the chairs. The loathsome refrigerator. Light, however, would be intolerable. Emiko blinked and blinked, a growing pressure building behind her ears. What was wrong with them? Now the syrup from breakfast and the macaroni from lunch were glued to plates, stink of milk heavy and sour. Blood thudded inside her ears. Emiko yanked the garbage next to the table and ripped the top off. Shoved the plates, cutlery, cups into the bin.

"There! There! There!"

The moon shone through the window. More than half. Less than three-quarters.

Tea, Emiko panted softly, she had come in to get some tea.

Her stomach clenched. A shiver of icy breath skated down her arms, her neck. A distant roar, chinook-warmed and relentless, the shadow of pine boughs rippled darkness in the moonlit room. Emiko cupped her hands around her elbows. So cold. How could it be? She peered at the thermostat, but it was almost twenty-five degrees Celsius. Was it broken? Emiko breathed and the condensation crystallized around her face. She stared in wonder, breathed in deeply, then blew out, a slow steady frozen stream that clouded her vision. The facets of ice seemed to hang in mid-air and she stared with a strange wonder at the brilliance in the tiny shards.

Her bedroom door squeaked as the furnace whooshed a small vacuum of air. And the creak creak of the loose hardwood in the hallway.

"Mommy?"

Emiko spun around. Oh! Her fingertips covering her trembling lips. She reached for the light switch but snatched back her hand. Darkness. Only the dark would call her back. Please.

A cry, forlorn.

"OhgodpleaseTara!" Emiko whispered fierce. It was all a mistake. A joke. A lesson and Emiko had learned. All was forgiven. Nothing was irreversible.

Emiko sank to the hardwood, arms outstretched. "Oh, baby. My best girl," she called, hot tears filling her eyes. An ache in her chest, her breasts. So familiar, a mother never forgot. She held her arms outstretched and shuffled in a slow circle. "Come here, my little kitten."

"Mommy?"

Outside! She was outside!

Emiko burst through the back door, the cracked glass breaking into shards beneath the palms of her hands. Jagged edges scraped up the soft skin of her forearms, but all Emiko could feel was warmth trickling, dripping off her elbows.

Where was she? Where?

"Tara, honey. Mommy's here. You come home now," Emiko cajoled. She ran about the backyard, the soak of slush and snow turning into mud. Her socks slipped and she fell to her hands and knees. Noticed the inside of her arms. The blood. The bad blood.

"Oh please," she gulped. "Come home."

A mewling cry.

Emiko held her breath.

The sound rose, angry, a hissing crescendo, a yowling spate screeching, howling.

"Huh, huh," Emiko panted.

Cats! Hal's goddamn Siamese cats, oh god, just cats. Emiko laughed. Choked.

She would kill them.

She squeezed wet snow and mud under her palms and threw it against Hal's fence. "Shut up!" she screamed, the dark handfuls splattering on the pale surface. "Shut up!"

A sudden movement behind her. Emiko spun around.

A hunched figure scurried away from the slats of her fence, scuttling up the alley with jerky bowed legs.

Emiko's eyes narrowed. It was *her*! Now she was spying! Who did she think she was staring into people's yards in the middle of the night? Silently, she rose from the muddy ground. Dashed across the lawn and down the dark lane.

The stranger's legs clattered, jerked up and down, limbs strung on string and Emiko splashed through dark puddles, feet numb with cold. Churned gravel and ice beneath her toes. Closer. Panting. She ran, arm reaching out. The air silent. The alley stretched long and skewed the line of naked poplars into a distorted horizon. The electrical lines plunged downward into the sky. Emiko panted hot, her heart thudding blood in her ears, slower, louder. Stretched her hand across the gap, squeezed a handful of the overcoat.

"Stop!" Emiko burst. Blood hot in her breath. Emiko jerked back, rough, and the stranger stumbled. Didn't turn around.

Emiko shook the woman's coat, but the stranger did nothing. Didn't turn to confront the person who held her, only jerked her legs up and down, trying to scurry away.

"What do you want?" Emiko hissed. "Why were you spying?"

The stranger said nothing. Feet splashing in a frenzy.

Why didn't she fight back? Emiko thought furiously. Why didn't she say anything?

"What's the matter?" she yelled. "Don't you speak English?" She shook her angrily. "Don't you?" Emiko released her grip and the woman almost stumbled to the ground. But she caught herself and clambered forward. Emiko grasped her arm through the thick material and tried to yank her around so she could scream in her face. But the stranger spun quickly away, refusing.

"Look at me!" Emiko sprayed. "It wasn't my fault! I don't know who told you! I couldn't see her! Do you understand? It was a mistake. She was playing in the alley!"

Emiko clung. The woman jerking from her gaze. If only Emiko could see her face, she could convince her. Please. Emiko's nails gave way beneath the rough material of the coat and as several flipped backwards, she screamed. The stranger broke from her grasp and scuttled in the opposite direction.

Emiko ran after the foreigner and darted in front of her, grabbed both arms. She began shouting into her face.

Stopped.

The woman.

Somehow she had turned around before Emiko had grabbed her, because Emiko held not her forearms, but her elbows. She was staring at the back of her head.

"Stop it!" Emiko hissed. "You face me!" Furious, Emiko yanked her around, never letting go of the heavy jacket, she clasped and released handfuls of cloth, back to elbow, elbow to the front lapel, but when the stranger had been turned 180 degrees, Emiko was still staring into the back of her head.

The hair on Emiko's arms, her neck turning to water, no, Emiko mouthed, no, how could this be?

Emiko spun the woman around, she must see her face. Faster and faster, Emiko spun the stranger, desperate to catch up, sobbing, her tears streamed into saliva, gulping to hold down her heart. But every way she turned her, the woman had no face.

She had no face.

Emiko dropped her shaking hands. Mouthing words without sound. She watched the stranger clatter away on puppet-string legs, walking away as she would always walk away.

Emiko turned and ran back toward her house. The alley churned mud and the fences were unfamiliar. She ran in her torn feet, the cold clinging to her limbs growing heavy with exhaustion. The alley stretched with a dreamy paleness and she ran, the ground slipping away from her steps, the fences unfurling slowly and eternally, her gasps and sobs becoming thinner and thinner.

"Emee-ko!"

For a moment, she didn't know what the sound meant.

"Emee-ko!"

She stopped and stared blankly.

Hal's white face peered over his back fence into the alley. His small eyes pouchy with sleep, his mouth hanging slightly open. "Oh my god!" He unhooked the latch of his gate and stumbled toward her.

Emiko looked down at her hands. Her inner arms were torn from elbows to wrists, blood caked dry and brown. Heat pulsed dimly in several fingers. She turned her hands around to stare at the missing fingernails and the beauty of the raw flesh speckled red and white. She could see. The sun had risen and the night was in someone else's heartbeat.

"Oh god, girl! You're okay. You're okay." Hal grabbed her and gave her a little shake. He opened his arms to enfold her, the scent of baby powder mixed with sour brine stench rising from his housecoat.

He smelled so bad, Emiko thought dimly. And her mouth dropped open to wail.

"There, there," Hal patted her head. "You cry now. You just let it all come out."

Emiko shook her head inside the stinking warmth of his humanity. Oh god! She had been so close. So close.

"M-m-my face!" Emiko gasped, shuddering with terrible fear. She sobbed, raising her tattered hands.

"Shhhh," Hal shushed, his small blue eyes earnest. "Your face doesn't have a mark. It looks right fine, don't worry your pretty head about that."

Emiko wailed even louder. The pain would last a very long time.

Camp Americana

"I'm not one to complain, but the Canadian stewardesses are much older than the ones on Japan Airlines. It just doesn't seem as safe. It's not about how attractive they are, you understand, but whether or not they have the strength to open the hatches and carry people out if need be. But then, what do I know?" Masahiro crosses his arms and stares at his middle-aged son.

Osamu automatically bobs his head.

"It's my turn!" Jennifer hisses in English at her older brother. She begged for a raccoon-skin Davy Crockett hat at the last gas station and now she never takes it off.

Masahiro's lips turn down. His grandchildren. They sit on the bench opposite, their comics, notepads, coloured pencils, and game cartridges spread all over the kitchen table. The girl with that ridiculous and filthy hat. Speaking in English in front of their visiting grandfather when they could try harder with their atrocious Japanese.

Gary turns his shoulder so his sister can't see the screen of his Gameboy. The sound is turned off because Ojī-chan complained about the noise.

"I *said*, It's *my turn!*"

"This is mine. You don't even know how to use the buttons right," Gary mumbles.

"It's not fair. I never get to play with it. Shizuko says we have to share!" Jennifer's eyes glint dark and bright. She deepens her voice. "Santa's watching. . . ."

Masahiro snorts. He can't understand their words but their tone is unmannered and disagreeable. And calling their mother Shizuko! What was the world coming to? How could Osamu let the wife drive this over-sized vehicle? Masahiro glares at his own wife asleep in the swivel chair next to the door, her mouth foolishly slack. Masahiro is certain that the medication Shizuko gave her must be sleeping pills, not anti-nausea tablets.

"And the food," Masahiro points his finger at his son, "American food is so bad. Not only is it overcooked and oversized, it's floating in oil and laden with salt."

"It's Canadian food," Osamu offers, "not American."

"Yes, Canadian. That's what I said. Canadian food is bad for you; it's making you fat and look at the size of your wife. Before long, your children will be fat too and their classmates will laugh at them. You understand?"

"Yes, Papa," Osamu monotones.

"There. I'm finished." Masahiro nods emphatically. Osamu closes his eyes, the flesh of his cheeks settling.

It's a long way to come just to visit grandchildren, Masahiro thinks, sighing. They talk in English to each other like foreigners and their Japanese so poor and such an accent! Grandchildren of his own blood and he cannot know them. And Gary. What a thing to name a child. What does it matter what Gary means in English? Gary was practically diarrhoea in Japanese. What could his son have been thinking?

Masahiro turns to glare at the grandchildren, but they ignore him.

"Stop breathing on my neck," Gary mutters to his sister. "It stinks."

"That's *my* book," Jennifer enunciates. "Why don't you just play with *your* Gameboy?"

"You weren't even looking at it."

"It's mine. Grandma gave it to *me*. Santa probably just wrote that down on his list. 'Gary steals books.'"

"I did not steal your book! I'm just looking at it."

Who would have thought that his son would throw away his own country and move to a land of foreigners? Masahiro shakes his head. Who would have thought he'd marry one? Her blood's Japanese, true enough, but her thinking is foreign through and through. Their children call the parents by their first names! "Shizuko," they chirp in public spaces, "Osamu!" The children throw their parents' names away and nothing good can come of that. And his son's wife. "Papa," she calls him. So familiar. Like they've eaten off the same plate. "Papa," she calls him, throwing that away as well. What the boy saw in her he really doesn't know. But his son always had a taste for things foreign.

"Shizuko!" Jennifer screeches. "A truck just passed us and the man was holding his dick!"

Masahiro makes pinching motions with his thumb and forefinger, adding a little twist to make it look even more painful. Jennifer scowls back, her irises so dark that the whites are barely visible. She pushes the sagging spaghetti straps of her tank top back up, tosses her head, the tail of the raccoon-skin hat flying through the air. She turns her face forty-five degrees, chin raised.

Insolent! Masahiro thinks. Not cute at all. Not like a normal six-year-old. Mark my words, she's going to turn out pregnant if a stop isn't put to her behaviour.

"Your grandma's sleeping, so be quiet!" Shizuko hollers back. "Don't say 'dick' and don't look at perverts."

Gary, belatedly, peers out the window.

Masahiro doesn't know what the yelling is about, but he knows that they shouldn't be yelling at all. His son's wife wasn't raised properly, that's obvious. And the same thing is happening with his grandchildren. He glares at the little beasts, but they ignore him. Gary, he decides, isn't so obnoxious, but then, the child might be a weakling. A boy ought not to be bossed around by a younger sister.

Jennifer, bored, pokes her brother's meaty ribs. Gary elbows back. Jennifer grits her teeth and yanks a handful of hair at the back of her brother's head. Tears fill the boy's eyes. He's not allowed to hurt his sister and she knows it.

"Shizuko," Gary gulps, "Jennifer's pulling my hair."

"Don't tattle," Shizuko scolds.

Masahiro grimaces. Ill-mannered, he thinks. The females of this country are uncivilized. Masahiro shifts on the bench cushion, too thin for his worn buttocks. Sighs. When did Mama get so old? Masahiro shakes his head. A man carries age far better than a woman, especially with jogging and eating plenty of vegetables. And after the age of forty, a man's got to dress well. Mama has been just a little too fond of sweets, but she's a hard worker. Not like that woman. She doesn't even wake up to cook a decent breakfast for her children and husband! Masahiro's eyes narrow.

The children eat cold cereal covered in sugars and fats and Osamu eats a banana. He's not a monkey! He might not be an especially clever boy, but he works hard like his Mama. No, that woman stays in bed as long as she can and saunters into the kitchen like she owns the world and asks, "Breakfast, something eat, did you?"

Masahiro knows people do things differently in different countries, but some things must be maintained so the world runs smoothly. A woman must honour her husband and care for him. Children must respect adults. And the man must behave with dignity and authority.

"Damare!" Masahiro bellows, startling the children, who hadn't been saying a thing.

Jennifer blinks her shock, her mouth working.

"See, did you sukebe in truck holding in hand pee pee?" Gary blurts in broken Japanese.

"WAAAAAAAAAA!" Jennifer bawls. She yanks her hat off and flings it across the camper, just missing her grandmother's head.

Gary thrusts the Gameboy toward his sister, but she knocks it away, inconsolable.

Shizuko gives Osamu a look in the rear-view mirror. Mama doesn't even twitch, and Gary stoically thrusts out his lower lip, pulls up his T-shirt so it completely covers his head.

Osamu digs around in the cooler.

"Here's a nectarine," he soothes, pressing the fruit into Jennifer's hands. "Now be quiet, stop bawling."

Jennifer wails harder and Masahiro's fingers clench. All the girl needs is a good smack, he thinks.

"Just wipe her face," Shizuko calls out. There's a surge forward and the engine of the Winnebago shudders. "She can't stop crying if her tears and runny nose are messing up her face!"

Osamu obediently wipes his daughter's face and she stops crying like magic.

"Will you share your nectarine with Grandpa?" Masahiro asks Jennifer sweetly in Japanese.

She thrusts out her chin, shakes her head. Gary nudges her below the table, but she shakes her head harder.

"Jennifer doesn't like to share her food," Osamu apologizes.

"She should learn how. It's for her own good, you understand."

Masahiro grabs the nectarine from Jennifer and splits the soft fruit open with his horny thumbnail. Jennifer shrieks like it's her own flesh.

"Oh lord," Shizuko mutters.

It takes several hours for Osamu to hook the trailer up to various outlets and drains. Masahiro watches suspiciously. Was his son sure that the toilet water wasn't hooked up to the kitchen hose?

Osamu thrusts out his lower lip. Follows the trail of lines and tubing with his finger.

"Didn't you get a book of directions?" Masahiro asks. "Americans are so careless. A rental agency should provide written instructions and translation for visiting tourists."

"Isn't Mama calling you?" Osamu asks.

Mama washes vegetables outside, in a basin. Masahiro can hear Shizuko rustling around inside the trailer. Probably eating snacks.

"Jennifer! Gary!" Shizuko yells through the mesh kitchen window as the children dart into the trees. "Don't chase those poor chipmunks. What would you do if you caught them? Eat them? Just leave them alone! Don't go too far! The sun's going to set soon."

Masahiro glares at Shizuko's noise, but she shuts the window with a decided snick.

"Wash those carrots and potatoes once more," Masahiro advises Mama. "We don't know where they came from."

Mama grunts and gets another basin of water from the hand-operated pump.

"We should cook outside so the frying meat won't stink up the inside of the camper, you understand," Masahiro announces.

Osamu walks up from behind the trailer, wiping his hands on his pants. He clears his throat. "Well, there's a kitchen in this unit for a reason, Papa. I don't see why –"

"I, for one, don't want to sleep in fried meat air."

Shizuko thumps the fridge door shut and stomps into the back of the camper. The plastic dishes in the cupboard clatter.

"And we're making curry rice. We'll smell curry for days and the heat will make it worse, you understand. You brought that portable stove. We can cook on the picnic table." Masahiro crosses his arms.

"Why don't you go for a walk. For your health," Mama suggests in her gentle voice. Her pale face glowing in the growing dusk.

"That's a very good idea. Bring up my appetite. The children shall come with me. They need the exercise. I'm only a retired dentist, but I know they are genetically inclined toward obesity, you understand. Regular walks might combat it. I say this not to be mean, but for their own welfare. There, I'm finished." Masahiro strides toward the sounds of the playground. His withered head vulnerable on top of a bony neck. He is swallowed up by the trees.

Jennifer screeches on the swing set and Gary, crouching, stares at the ground.

Jennifer stretches and bends her knees, pumping higher and higher. The tail of the raccoon hat trailing behind her. She spits and the white gob arcs, splats near her brother's feet. She shrieks gleefully.

"Shizuko!" Gary yells automatically.

"Oi! Oi!" Masahiro points his finger at the girl. "That's no behaviour for a little girl! Come down off that swing and apologize to me and your brother!"

Jennifer pumps higher and higher, toes reaching toward the tips of the cedar and spruce. On the final rise of an arc, she launches her body out of the swing and hangs in mid-air. The background a frieze of exposed branches, undergrowth.

Masahiro's heart plummets, then balloons inside his chest. His arms stretch out as if he can catch her, but she floats in slow motion far beyond his reach.

Red dust clouds upon impact. Surely she has broken her spine. But Jennifer adjusts her hat, brushes off her filthy shorts, and marches back through the trees, raccoon tail swinging. Masahiro's mouth flaps for words. The child disappears and a few moments later he hears the screen door smack.

"You!" he manages. "You!"

A hot dry hand curls into his palm.

Gary stares past Masahiro's head. Masahiro looks over his shoulder, but he cannot see anything except the darkening trees. He shakes his head. What is the world coming to? Girls jumping out of swings, boys who are crybabies.

"Come on, boy. I have an odometer feature on my wristwatch. Let's see how long it takes you to walk five kilometres."

"I'm goin' cra-zy," Shizuko sings in English, her voice sunny, the melody of "On Top of Ol' Smoky."

The children giggle from the recessed bunk above the cab of the camper.

> "I'm going mad!
> Why do I bear this?
> He's your friggin' Dad!
> Why don't we leeeave him,
> in a well forested place,
> Your mom will thank me
> I would in her place!"

The children giggle again and Jennifer sings too.

"I'm going *cra-zy!*"

"Don't, Shizuko. You'll encourage the children," Osamu whispers.

"Jennifer! Take off your hat. Time to sleep, no singing. And Shizuko was just joking," Shizuko says.

Osamu sighs. Squiggles around the small ledge of a bed that he and Shizuko share. It doesn't seem right that they'll dismantle the bed tomorrow and call it a kitchen table. Then eat off it. Osamu sighs again. Sex is out of the question.

"I'm serious, Osamu," Shizuko whispers. "You have *nooo* idea what your father does to me! If you don't get him to shut up, I can't be blamed for my actions."

"How can the man change? He's been like this his whole life. It's only until the end of August. Please."

Shizuko opens her mouth to say something, but pinches it tight instead. She kisses Osamu on the cheek and rolls over to face the door.

"You're lucky I love you so much," she hisses.

So inconsiderate, Masahiro thinks. Tugs more blanket from Mama, not used to sharing. Singing so loudly, yelling. Other campers will hear and she can't even carry a tune. The children are probably tone deaf by now.

Mama's breathing is a cool whistle, like an autumn wind blowing the last leaves off bare-limbed trees. Her white face cold. Masahiro jabs his thumb into her side and Mama rolls over. Masahiro sighs. He could be golfing in the Rockies or swimming in a properly chlorinated pool at a resort hotel. But, no, camping in a used camper with an ill-mannered fat woman and uncivilized children. A weakling for a son. Who knows what kind of family had the camper before them? What manner of germs, viruses, and bacteria? A retired dentist ought not to find himself on such a low-class holiday!

What could that boy have been thinking, taking a seventy-five-year-old man on a camping trip? Why not just go white-water rafting and be done with it? Not that he feels weak and decrepit. But a man his age must be treated with certain respect and honour. Tomorrow, tomorrow, he will disinfect all of the cutlery with his rubbing alcohol. They'll have to stop at a drug store to get some more. Tomorrow, Masahiro nods sleepily.

Tomorrow, Masahiro shudders, how quickly it comes. He is icy to the core and a dull pressure balloons in his bladder. He gropes futilely for the covers. Mama has curled up inside the quilt and Masahiro is left with nothing. The inside of his mouth a sour pit, he smacks his lips, the chapped skin rasping like husks of insects. He shivers and the reverberations amplify inside his bladder. Certainly he cannot wait until morning. Beer is not meant to be consumed while camping, Masahiro decides.

He slides his hand along the small shelf next to the bed for his glasses. When he puts them on the dim night shapes becomes less ominous. That heap of monstrous snoring is the boy's foreign wife. That otherworldly grinding is the weakling grandson's teeth. He'll have to check them in the morning. That boy is a prime candidate for a retainer.

Where has that woman put the flashlight! It should be placed right next to the door in case of emergencies, urinary or otherwise. There is the camper-trailer toilet, but he will not be using it. He's still not sure if Osamu put all of the hoses in the right places. Also, his and Mama's bed is right next to the bathroom. He would smell urine all night. No, there is a perfectly good outhouse and Masahiro will do his business there.

Masahiro slips his feet into Osamu's rubber slippers. Hips aching, he raises his bony buttocks from the thin mattress and shuffles to the door, his hand held out in front of him. The full moon shines through the dusty curtains outlining the rounded bulk of his sleeping son and his wife. The children in the bunk-shelf above the driver's seat. The grinding noise stops. Does a head lift?

Masahiro peers, but the bunk space recesses into a dark rectangle.

"Oi," Masahiro says hoarsely. Maybe one of the children could take him to the outhouse.

A vacuum of sound.

Pachi. Pachi.

No. He hasn't imagined it, for certain! One of the children is awake. Staring at him. Blinking. He can hear the moist sound of eyelids closing, opening.

"Get down here and help your grandfather," Masahiro demands, but his voice ends on a querulous wobble.

No one answers.

The air stills. The breathlessness uncanny. Like he's in a room filled with corpses. Masahiro exhales jaggedly through his nostrils. A rush of shivery hair rises, blooms across his back. "Heh, heh," he manages. Shakes his head at his nighttime folly. The disrespectful lot of them. He will go to the outhouse by himself.

Masahiro shuffles to the screen door and squeezes the twist latch in his bony fingers. Pulling briskly, the latch squeaks, but the door doesn't budge. He twists harder, but only a dry screeech; the door does not pull open. Scree! Scree! He twists and twists again, the door refusing. Experimentally, he turns the knob more slowly, with careful concentration.

CREEEEEEEEEEECH.

"OhforChrissake!"

Hands thrust him aside and the screaming door is flung outward and open. Sweet cold night air slides into the moist heat of their shared air. Masahiro coughs and vapour balloons into his hot face. An icy kiss. Shizuko lumbers back onto the kitchen table bed. The legs squeal beneath her weight.

Masahiro peers out into the night. No one is offering to guide him to the outhouse despite the fact that he's seventy-five years old and his night vision has been greatly reduced. Not that he is old and incompetent, but if that woman hasn't the manners to offer her company, she ought to know enough to enlist one of the children.

Not that he's frightened of going himself.

Masahiro grabs the door frame and taps out the steps. Fallen leaves, dry twigs break crackle beneath his feet like dead insects.

He should have worn a coat. The forest night is as cold as winter in Nagoya. The warmth is sucked from his lungs, and, unbidden, he thinks of the Woman of the Snow. Her deathly kiss. Heh, heh. When has he become so fanciful? His chest aches. But he won't go back into the camper for that woman to think he's witless and forgetful.

Which way is the outhouse?

Masahiro peers about. The conifers are unnaturally tall. Masahiro blinks hard, squints a slow circumference. The moon slips among clouds, black and roiling. Spotlights fixed on to electrical posts cast pallid cones of unearthly light throughout the grounds. His son's managed to choose the only camper pad that's completely surrounded by trees. He supposes an American would just pull out his member and do his business on the ground with no thought to children walking about the next day. Masahiro is not beyond temptation, but expedience is no excuse for uncivilized behaviour no matter what the circumstances. Why, he'd be no better than an animal.

When the moon slides out of the clouds, he can catch glimpses of the damp picnic table, the fire-pit, and Masahiro shuffles around them. The pale gravel reflects a strange greenish glow and he crunches over the surface. The drive must lead to the main road and then there would signs. Masahiro peers down at his feet, stepping carefully. A fall at his age could easily cause broken bones.

His breath puffs moistly against his cheeks.

Tiny flecks of lights in the branches. Masahiro is not sure if it's an optical illusion. He rubs his eyelids with his pinkies, gently, in a circular motion. The minute motes flicker. Open, shut. They crowd close, blinking. Masahiro drops his gaze, curls his brittle hands over his icy arms. Heh, heh, he manages. Fireflies, of course. The cold presses his bladder, a painful weight.

"Ehhhhh," something groans.

Masahiro twists around, his back popping. He stares into the black-limbed trees. Are leaves rustling? Did something move?

The night air creaks the thick waists of trees, a keening whistle slides through heavy branches.

The hollow booming of his heart echoes in his eardrums.

The jumbled bones of undergrowth, crisscrossing boughs of trees all shapes and flickering bits of light. Eyes. Mist rising. A hollow of warmth. Did something breathe?

A small hump of shadow. At the base of a tree. There! It moved! He is certain of it! The rounded shape of a head, tilting to one side. On its haunches. It's staring and staring and Masahiro cannot move. And the night. An inaudible mechanical *click*. He feels the sound against his face. On his skin.

One of the spotlights has gone out.

Hoarse air rasps his throat. He is breathing loudly enough for all to hear. He cannot move to save his life.

Click.

"Ohhhh," he moans.

The pallid cones of light disappear. One after the other.

Click.

Click.

The forest consumes him. The darkness enfolds his skinny form and he cannot inhale. Like when breath-sucking night haunts sit upon his chest, Masahiro is paralyzed.

Icy, bony fingers slide across Masahiro's palm and clamp down, hard, across his hand. The faintest prickle of pointed nails.

His feet are stuck to the earth. His thighs and calves calcified into stone, he feels the creeping deadness twine up his torso. . . . He is not ready to go.

Frantically, he flings his scrawny arm, flailing wildly and the deathly cold hand loses its grip. Panting, whimpering, he lurches in the direction of the camper; the rubber slippers skewing away from his heels, he stumbles. And with an agility born of desperation, he flips them off his feet. One! Two! His slippers fly through the air. He pitches forward, his arms swing in vain windmills, the gravel biting the side of his face. His glasses flip off into the night. He falls to the ground as if he had been thrown.

Click.

He cannot distinguish the camper from the trees.

He is not ready. No. Please. Whatever it is that he must endure. Let it pass from him tonight. Masahiro grits his teeth between prayer and curses.

Then.

An orange light flicks on in the night. Distant, but close enough he can see the shape. Rectangular. A window. Someone is awake. They must have missed him. Worried. They will come for him! Masahiro waves his arm wildly. "Oiiii!" he shouts. "Oiiiiiii!"

"Shut up." A voice. A childish voice. Sweet and cold as winter air.

Masahiro flinches. Then releases his breath. A warm waft clouds his face.

"Jenny-fah!" Masahiro laughs. "Jenny-fah!"

The little bitch. He will put on a good face now and make sure she's punished tomorrow. "Oji-chan's had a little fall." He turns toward her. "Go get –"

"I said," Jennifer's voice enunciates in English, "shut up."

The words cool, distinct.

Her head. It's . . . overlarge. Masahiro blinks and blinks. He cannot focus. "Heh, heh," he manages. That stupid American hat. Without averting his gaze, he pats the forest floor for his glasses. Her eyes glow green. A trick of light or his sight. Her eyes loom larger, closer and she is upon him, her fetid breath in his face, her cold wet nose pressed against his. She licks his cheek. Rasps. Her coarse tongue will tear his skin. He bats at her head and his hand glances off soft fur, but the hat. . . . She leaps away and stands nonchalantly, her pale arm and legs glowing. She is outlined in the moon. He blinks rapidly. Can almost make out triangular ears, a feline head, on Jennifer's childish body.

"Leave him alone," a boy sighs from behind him.

"Gary!" Masahiro blinks back tears. So suddenly. Surely, he loves his grandson. "Gary, my boy!" Masahiro cranes his head back.

Into the muzzle of a fat cat.

The boy is wearing his housecoat. Pyjama bottoms. But his head. His face. Gary's troubled eyes stares at him from a cat face.

"Ehhhhhh," Masahiro moans. A hot pool grows rapidly cold in the crotch of his pyjamas.

"Jesus!" Jennifer leaps further back.

"Oh, Oji-chan!" Gary mutters. He reaches down for his grandfather's hand.

Masahiro does not want his touch. But the other cat is a bristling presence. He can feel her distemper emanating from her skin. Her furred face. Masahiro puts his trembling fingers into his grandson's palm. The boy's hand is hot and dry.

"Here to come you shouldn't have," Gary explains wearily in Japanese. "For us tonight important."

"I never wanted to go camping!" Masahiro blurts. "I never liked the wilds. I like wildlife, you understand. Ecosystems. Very important. Balance. Heh, heh, heh."

The pain is fast and keen. It slices, dissipates, then blooms across his back. Masahiro gasps.

The monstercat licks her fingers. Instead of human nails, retractable claws curl from the pink tips.

"Stop it, Jennifer!" Gary snaps. "I mean it."

"It's just a little scratch. What are you going to do?" Jennifer coos. "Tell Shizuko?"

Could he try creeping away? Masahiro whispers to himself. While they fight? If they turned upon each other he could run for the camper. Ohhhh, what manner of children are they? Their mother is a monster. His fool son. His poor, poor son would blame himself for his father's death. But Shizuko would say Papa must have wandered off, senile. Hypothermia. Masahiro sniffles. Something rattling in his throat.

"Kora!" a stern voice calls out. From the darkness.

Oh!

Relief is a soft breeze; a kiss releasing the clench of terror held in his jaws, shoulders. His groin. Masahiro's heart lifts. His whole life he has been saved from the daily indignities. His socks, underwear pressed and laid out on the bed. The bread toasted while he brushed his teeth. The deliveries and pickup arranged, and he had never paid a bill in his entire life. Food appearing like it ought to whenever he was hungry. His bath filled until it ran over. Abundance and grace. His life path has been polished and shined by his helpmate, Mama, all along.

He pushes against the ground. Feels the cold circles of his glasses against his fingertips. They are intact and he eagerly perches them on his nose.

"Chiye. You heard me." He turns, a smile breaking his face in half. "These children – these monst –"

His wife.

Her face.

It bobs mere inches from his. Lit up like a paper lantern, her face glows. Her expression is benign. She stares at him. Small black eyes unblinking. Like they are painted on her skin. He cannot feel her breathing. Her breath.

Masahiro cannot move.

His wife's head starts weaving. Churning, moiling through the night air, his wife's neck writhes sinuously without a sound.

Her body, sitting neatly on the ground, is three metres away.

Masahiro's cells. They scream inside his body. Blood turning sluggish, thickening, icy, and his limbs lock, turn to stone.

His wife. His wife.

Has she been a monster all along?

Masahiro cannot bear it. His heart convulses erratic, a hiccup of pain stutters, spasms inside his chest. The defining edges of sight decay. A mist swells from the periphery. Ever closer. Rising from the mouldy leaves, the clammy soil. He can hear Jennifer laughing. A mewling sound. If he closes his eyes, it will all go away.

"Yes," his wife's face mouths. Her sagging cheeks are fuller, but not with blood. Her lantern face glows. Her lips black in the darkness. "That's right."

Starts twining her serpentine neck around his frozen body.

"So bad he's not," Gary says, his voice muffled. Masahiro can barely hear him.

"Don't be stupid!" Jennifer hisses in English, but the rest of what she says is lost.

His wife's neck winds round and round. Her skin is cold. Stink of wet iron. Bumpy and rough like the skin of a giant Gila monster, her neck scrapes against his hands, his arms, slowly rising toward his face. Coil after coil. Squeezing tight his heart. The cold. So cold. His nerves jerk, twitch inside his body. His mouth falls open in a howl. But no sound comes out. His face screams, silent.

"Hey! Shhhhht! Shhhhhh!"

A staccato of clapping hands.

Masahiro is released so suddenly that he slumps to the forest floor. The ground darts with frightened motion. It leaps, darts, slithers in different directions.

Masahiro stares blankly at the leaf litter in front of his face. The smell of decay is tinged with smoke. A pair of swollen human feet stops before him. The dawn is coming. For he can make out the plump toes. The person scrunches down and a huge nightgown balloons open to reveal a fragrant crotch. Luminous panties. She smells like the beach and lavender soap.

"Papa!" Shizuko shouts. "Papa! Okay, are you?"

Such a stupid question, Masahiro thinks. Such a stupid woman. Hot tears slide sideways across his face. He can't move.

"Osamu!" Shizuko roars. "Osamu!"

The sound of pounding steps. Breaking branches. Osamu's sleep-encrusted eyes blink and blink. He presses his face so close that Masahiro could kiss him if he could move his lips.

"Papa?" Osamu quavers. Masahiro stares back.

"Maybe he had a stroke," Shizuko's voice whispers. Her toes squeeze anxiously. They are calloused and unattractive. "There were animals around him! No! Don't try to move him." Masahiro can hear someone starting to blubber.

"He might have broken something," Shizuko continues hoarsely. "How long was he out here? He's wet himself. The poor thing." She lumbers to her feet. The waft of her crotch is pungent. Masahiro can hear his son bawling like a baby.

"Does anyone know first aid?" Shizuko bellows to the early dawn. "Does anyone know first aid?"

Masahiro wishes he could close his eyes.

There is a crunch of branches snapping. Childish feet in thongs stop in front of his frozen gaze.

"What happened to Ojī-chan?" a tremulous voice asks.

Indignation, outrage flickers deep inside Masahiro's rib cage, but the movement is as small as a dying sparrow. He doesn't have the energy to sustain the emotions.

"Shhhhh, don't worry," Shizuko consoles. "Someone!" she bellows to the skies. "Ojī-chan is really old, Jenny-love," she continues in a loud whisper. "He's not feeling well. But we'll get help. Gary, go wake up your grandmother."

"I'm s-s-sorry," Gary stammers. Masahiro can hear real tears in the boy's throat. A residual warmth glows. I don't blame you, boy.

"What are you sorry for?" Shizuko scolds affectionately. Osamu hasn't stopped blubbering. "Go get your grandmother. We have to let her know."

No! Masahiro wants to shout. No, not that. He can feel the ties to his body beginning to fade. Strand by strand, the pull of earth and life seems to fall off his spirit. But it is not fast enough.

The boy's pudgy feet trot out of his sight.

Hurry this release, Masahiro pleads. He'd rather die than look upon Chiye's face.

Jennifer peers sideways at him, directly into his eyes. "Really?" she asks. "Want that, do you?" She looks perfectly normal.

"Don't, sweetie," Shizuko says. Her large hand clamps on her daughter's bony shoulder.

"Ojī-chan says he'd rather die than look at Obā-chan."

"No! Why would he say such at thing?" Shizuko stares, open-mouthed, at her daughter. Jennifer shrugs carelessly. Shizuko drops to her knees and enunciates her words, yelling like Masahiro is at the end of a long tunnel. "Hear – us – can – you, Papa?" she shouts in his face. Shizuko turns to her daughter. "Did he say why, sweetheart?" she whispers hoarsely.

Masahiro can hear the dragging shuffle of his wife's gait coming closer and closer. He had thought that her shoddy way of walking had been caused by the overuse of slippers inside the house. Did he remember a time when she had walked differently?

"Papa!" Shizuko shouts, "you – want – to – go, okay – it – is!"

"Nooooo," Osamu moans.

Something twinges in Masahiro's chest. He had no idea that his son had cared for him at all. Osamu, you've been a good son to me, he lies.

"He's lying that you've been a good son," Jennifer relays.

Shizuko gasps. "That's just like him! You really can hear!"

"Masahiro-san?" Chiye's voice sounds old and fragile. His skin would be crawling if it could. Her faltering footsteps shuffle through the dead leaves, the damp air smells of early rot.

The cool morning sun breaks through the spruce and pine and pale golden beams slant across Masahiro's body. As if he has been called by the promise of warmth, Masahiro's ether slowly seeps out of his earthbound shell. The cold paralysis left lying on top of the forest debris, Masahiro rises with the mist, drifting upward on warming currents of air. His ether passes through branches of pine and spruce. The memory of touch tickles.

"Goodbye, then," Jennifer whispers. The girl tilts her head to one side, an unreadable expression on his granddaughter's face. Then she purses her lips and blows hard. The blast of warm air catches Masahiro and he's tossed upward. Flung into somersaults and spirals, he finds a still pocket of air above his family. Hovering, he stares down at the tableau below him. It looks like a movie, he thinks. He can see Osamu's bald head bobbing with sorrow. Fat Shizuko dwarfs his freak wife who may or may not be the Chiye he married so very long ago. Gary, crouching down next to his body, looks like he is praying. Only Jennifer looks up. Her dark eyes glint in the rising sun. Chiye follows Jennifer's gaze. Her mouth drops open in a wail.

So many years, Masahiro thinks. So much time.

"Anata!" his wife's thin voice wails across a separate reality.

But the sun burns off the damp of night and Masahiro's ether floats ever lighter, transparent.

Masahiro bobs, rises, a forward-backward drifting like a feather falling upward.

The sun is bright, a loud invitation. He rises toward its call. Really, he thinks, his entire life. He hadn't known any of them at all.

Hopeful Monsters

Goldschmidt did not object to general microevolutionary principles, how-ever, he veered from the synthetic theory in his belief that a new species develops suddenly through discontinuous variation, or macromutation. He agreed that most macromutations ended disastrously, with what he called "monsters." Nonetheless, Goldschmidt believed that a small percent-age of macromutations could, with chance and luck, equip an organism with radically beneficial adaptive traits with which to survive and pros-per. These he called "hopeful monsters". . . .

Hisa started experiencing nausea the third week after fertilization and tested positive in the fourth. She couldn't eat anything in the mornings and had to forego her single cup of coffee, but by two-thirty in the afternoon, her stomach had settled enough for a bowl of plain congee at the Golden Garden Café. By then, the noon line-up had disappeared and she partook of her rice porridge in peace. She ate meditatively. She never brought a book.

Junko, her mother, phoned every day.

"After you give birth, you must bind your loose belly with a long cloth. This will help you get your figure back."

Hisa wound her finger into the spirals of the telephone cord. She had switched back from the cordless after she kept losing the unattached receiver. She didn't bother bringing up the fact that she never had much of a figure to begin with. Bobby didn't mind, she reassured herself. Bobby's belly was as big as hers and they joked about it when they lay in bed, naked.

"This is your first baby," Junko continued. "You must have good thoughts. Bad thoughts will travel down the umbilical tube and affect the baby."

"It's an umbilical cord," Hisa murmured.

"And don't you fight with Bobby. The bad energy might cause your baby to have psychological problems."

Hisa didn't know whether her mother spoke out of superstition or experience.

"I wanted to have four babies, but I went through hard times and didn't I lose three of them, one after the other?"

Hisa imagined her mother setting her baby in the sales bin of the downtown Hudson's Bay department store. As she rifled through oversized and over-handled panties, clacked swiftly through one-piece dresses, elastic-waisted pants, and out-of-style skirts, the baby squirmed in the bed of soft panties, the silky cloth parting like water. He sank slowly and surely until he was completely covered.

"Mama, you had miscarriages. Lots of women do." To be on the safe side Hisa crossed her fingers, knocked on the kitchen cabinet, and silently offered a quick prayer to God for the well-being of her child.

"And didn't you turn out soft in the head?" Junko continued. "Not a backbone in you, it's a wonder you had sense enough to get married."

Hisa sighed. But her mother, still talking, didn't hear her.

By the beginning of her third trimester, she was retaining quite a bit of water. Not to worry, her family physician said. Blood pressure's fine and your weight gain within normal range. Lots of women retained water. Something about cells and amniotic fluid. Hisa didn't care as long as it wasn't dangerous and went away after the delivery. She was thirty-one years old.

"We're mostly water anyway," he chuckled. The hairs on his hands distracted her so she closed her eyes.

"Mmmm," she said.

"A little more won't do you harm and when the water breaks, down will come baby, cradle and all, ha, ha, ha."

Was that a joke? Hisa wondered. It wasn't funny. She must have frowned because Dr Armstrong cleared his throat. "There. All done. You're looking great. Have you been doing your pelvic exercises? I'll see you in two weeks. If you have any prolonged pain that goes beyond Braxton Hicks or any sign of bloody discharge, phone your symptoms to our nurse. There's nothing to worry about."

"Should I be worried?" Hisa asked, opening her eyes.

The fluorescent light buzzed around Dr Armstrong's shiny head. His pale blue eyes were vague. Like the kind that Hisa had seen on some white horses. She'd never liked white horses. She wondered if milky eyes were one of those things that happened to men more than women, like that bleeding disease. She couldn't remember. She had studied Restoration Literature at university, but she *had* been fond of biology when she was in high school.

"Now what can there be to worry about? You're about to embark on the most natural journey of life. A commonplace miracle. Ha, ha, ha."

Hisa closed her eyes again. Dr Armstrong was Bobby's doctor. She kept her eyes shut through the last of his commentary and reopened them only after his shoes squeaked through the door. Hisa stared at the bulge that rose magnificently from her midriff. The baby churned, digging a knee or elbow. She could see her skin give, as if an alien was trying to burst out of her belly even while she watched: alive and horrified. Ridley Scott had a lot to answer for, she thought. She wondered if he ever had to fight a lawsuit for causing maternal psychological trauma. Americans, she knew, sued over things like spilled coffee and music videos with homosexual male police officers. She used to think male doctors were so dependable and fatherly. Maybe it was those shows she watched as a child. *Trapper John, M.D. Marcus Welby. Quincy.* No, he was a coroner. She'd never go to a midwife, though. Midwifery sounded like something out of the Middle Ages. As Hisa shrugged into her clothes she decided she would look for a new doctor if she had another baby.

Hisa wasn't entirely certain when she went into labour. The small twinges of pain might have been gas or wishful thinking. Brow furrowed, she stared at the island of her belly. She just wanted to have her body back, thank you very much, and begin being a mother. She'd grown her hair long for the occasion. She would pin it up in a bun.

"Do you think it's started?" Bobby asked her belly. He was kneeling on the floor and when he raised his head to look earnestly at Hisa's face, his wetly beaded forehead shone with worry and excitement. They'd met at a wine-tasting workshop for singles. They dated for seven months before having sex.

Well. . . ." Hisa rubbed her stomach. That little twinge came again. A little muscle spasm. Or a gurgle of gas. Please, God, let it all be okay, she prayed silently. Hisa breathed deeply through her nose.

"I'm gonna call Mama," Bobby said, lurching to his feet. "Mama will know."

"Ohhh, Bobby. Mama might get it into her head to come over."

"Then she could help us!" Bobby thumped to the telephone in the kitchen, then thumped back. He stood in front of Hisa, clutching his teddy bear tummy. He was wearing his yukata again. The dark blue one he had taken from the hot spring hotel in Tō-yama.

Hisa bit her lip. She used to think he was so cute for wanting to wear it. Bobby wore his yukata so much the cloth was starting to unravel. She didn't have the heart to tell him that he reminded her of, who was it in that Clavell novel, turned into a TV miniseries? Richard Chamberlain! Hisa shuddered delicately. Though she didn't mind Bobby's beard so much. It hid his receding chin.

"Sweetheart, are you cold?" Bobby threw an afghan over her midriff and rubbed her hands. She was actually quite warm, but Bobby was sweet. Sweet as cotton candy. She would keep him even if he wore yukatas for the rest of his life. Bobby was forty-three.

"I'm fine," Hisa decided. "I'm going to go check my panties for any bloody discharge." She turned to her side and managed to get on to all fours. Crawled off the side of the bed. Bobby cupped her elbow. She felt mildly annoyed. Cupping her elbow didn't support any weight and she *knew* where the bathroom was. She lurched from side to side, her great belly leading the way.

While she was sitting on the toilet, Hisa heard the phone ring. "Don't answer it!" she called out. But Bobby was already murmuring. He trotted over with the phone in hand. The cord pulled taut from the hallway.

"You're in labour, aren't you?" Junko demanded.

"Mama, I'm on the toilet."

"I know you're in labour," Junko continued. "I was just laying down on the couch for a bit of relax when I felt a contraction. It started in my lower back and rippled across my belly. A mother never forgets. It's the umbilical tube," she whispered hoarsely. "Even though the doctors cut it at birth, the psychic tube is still intact. I can even feel my other babies. Not like I feel you," she added hurriedly. As if Hisa might be jealous. "But I feel all of my babies. I know."

Hisa tried to push away the image of dead babies floating in the ether around her mama's axis. Attached by lengths of milky tubing. "Goodness, Mama," she managed to laugh. "All the innocents go to heaven. They're not haunting you." Though she wasn't sure what happened to unblessed Catholic babies. . . .

"You're right," Junko said, smartly. "Nice thoughts. Nice words. I'll be right over."

"Mama, I —"

The line was dead.

"Baw-beeeeeee!" Hisa wailed. She lurched to her feet and pulled up her panties. Bloodless. She trundled through the hallway, dropped the phone into the cradle, then trudged into the living room where her husband was biting his fingernails. "Now Mama's coming over. I didn't w —"

Liquid gooshed between her legs, as if someone had burst a giant water balloon. Dousing her chubby thighs and streaming down the insides of her calves, a rich moist aroma filled the air. Hisa stared at the huge puddle.

"Oh, god," Bobby groaned. "Are you okay? Do you need to lie down?" His face was the colour of bathroom putty.

Hisa tapped one blue sock in the puddle, testing the temperature and consistency. "Goodness," she said. "There's so much! I wonder what colour that is." The hue was hard to make out on the hard wood floor.

A knife spasmed in her lower back then ricocheted in her uterus, right below her protruding belly button. So sudden. And the scale. Nothing in her life had prepared her for such pain. She screamed. As the lightning spasm dissipated, tears filled her eyes and ran down her cheeks.

"Mama's right," she bawled.

"Let's go. Let's go, let's go!" Bobby threw the afghan around Hisa's shoulders and bustled her into slippers. He snatched up her clutch purse with one paw, the keys with the other, and crammed a pillow into his armpit. He rushed her outside, the summer sun stabbing pupils into pinpricks. Hisa groped for the door of their two-door Toyota hatchback. They couldn't afford a second-hand Volvo, though they had wanted one for the safety of the baby. Bobby eased Hisa into the seat and crammed the pillow in front of her belly so that the baby wouldn't be crushed in a car accident.

Just as Bobby backed out of their driveway, the second contraction came lapping toward Hisa like the waves of an irrepressible ocean.

Hisa started wailing.

They had forgotten to bring everything they were supposed to bring. Most importantly, the hospital card.

"My water broke," Hisa cried.

"How far apart are your *contractions*?" the nurse asked. She inflected some of her words. Hisa didn't know if the nurse did it because she didn't think Hisa understood English or because people in the labour and delivery unit had trouble listening.

"My water broke," Hisa repeated.

"Maybe five minutes apart?" Bobby guessed. He wiped his shiny forehead with the back of his hand. He was still in his indigo yukata.

"Are you her husband?" the nurse asked.

"I'm the father." Bobby said sternly.

"Fill in these forms." The nurse turned to Hisa. "You're not going to *have* the baby, yet, sweetie. Your cervix has to be dilated *ten centimetres*, and that'll take some time if this is your *first baby*. Just *breathe* like you learned at prenatal class. Some women find that walking helps with the *pain*."

Hisa couldn't remember a thing she'd learned in the prenatal class. All she could remember was the lesbian couple. Maggie was the one who was pregnant. Hisa had wondered how they had decided who would carry. She would have thought Julia with her feminine looks and soft voice would have been the obvious choice. Maggie was curt and, well, she had hairy arms. But after one of the husbands had made a joke about turkey basters and bulls, Hisa had made a point of being extra nice to the lesbian couple. Hisa no longer went to church religiously, but she had taken the New Testament to heart and abided with its loving philosophy. When Hisa phoned after the classes had concluded, however, the lesbians didn't return the call. Hisa supposed they weren't Christians.

Hisa huffed and puffed like the little engine that could. She didn't want to walk, but she didn't want the nurse to think she was a baby. She tottered a few steps away from the nurse's station. Her right foot felt sticky inside her slipper.

A contraction keened into her belly, twisted through her abdomen, and breached her mouth. Her piercing scream filled the delivery unit.

The nurse hustled over with a wheelchair. Hisa didn't want to sit. She clutched the arms of the wheelchair, trying to keep her bottom off the seat. The nurse whisked her down long halls the colour of cream mints. Hisa screamed the whole way. Mouth wide open, her voice trailing behind her like a red banner, Hisa careened down the long hallways, astonished faces popping in and out of her sight, the fluorescent lights brief bright rectangular glares.

A tiny portion of Hisa's brain observed the scene dispassionately. You're overreacting. Women have given birth before. Do you want to look like an idiot?

"When I was going through labour," Mama had said, "I clamped down on a towel with my teeth and didn't scream at all. My eyes, though," her mother had conceded, "almost popped out of my head."

Hisa screamed even louder.

"I want to push!" she sobbed. "I want to push!"

"No!" the nurse snapped. "You must not push yet."

"Mmmmphh! Unnnnhhhhh!" Hisa swallowed her contractions until they ebbed away. Her body flopped in the wheelchair like a sack of rice.

"Baby," Bobby patted her with his sweat-damp hand. Hisa didn't know if he meant her or the one trying to come out of her. She jerked her arm away.

"I want my mama," Hisa sobbed.

Bobby was hurt. And his legs were getting chilled because his yukata was too short.

"We're just going to get you into a birthing room," the nurse chirped. She turned smartly on her rubber-soled white shoes and parked the wheelchair next to a table with stirrups. She helped Hisa onto the delivery table. Hisa obediently positioned her body, her feet in the padded foot-rests, her knees raised and parted. She looked a like fowl ready for basting. The contractions started lapping toward her again, faster, quicker, the pain punching one on top of the other.

"Lord Jesus! I wanna push!" Hisa screamed.

The nurse held Hisa's face still with both hands. Eyes blazing, her voice was as sharp as slaps. "You must not push. You'll rip yourself. You'll hurt the baby. Breathe until it passes!"

Bobby was beside her. He leaned close to whisper encouragement into her ear, telling her to breathe, two, three, four, and Hisa threw her right arm over his shoulder and around his neck. Squeezed him in a headlock as she bore the pain. Bobby's face purpled as she clamped harder and harder.

"Nnnnnnnnnnnnnnphhhhh," Hisa writhed and moaned. It felt like the biggest poop in her life was bursting to come out, but she was being told to hold it in. "Gimme the drugs!" she gasped. "I want the drugs now!" Suddenly there were more people in the room. A clear plastic mask was placed over her nose and mouth. Hisa released her death grip on Bobby's neck and he nearly fell to his knees. Hisa clutched the mask desperately with both hands and greedily sucked and sucked.

Only oxygen!

"Breathe slowly!" someone snapped. "You're going to hyperventilate and lose consciousness."

Hisa breathed as slowly as she could. Another contraction started pummeling her again. Tears ran down her face. Stars burst inside the spotlight that hung from the ceiling. The glare burned closer, closer, and as Hisa turned her face away, the light receded to a pinprick in a long hollow room. Voices muddied fast and loud.

"The baby's crowning! Who was the one – Baby! Hisa. I'm right here – You're in the way, please step – Push, now! Push!"

Hisa pushed and pushed. She held her breath, pushing down with her abdominal muscles, a squirt of residual fecal matter forced along as well, she pushed, pain no longer a sensation but an entity, and the bulk of baby head squeezed out millimetre after millimetre, until once past the nose, the rest of the head came easily and stopped at the neck. The baby's head collared by Hisa's vagina. Hisa gave one more valiant push and the rest of the body came slithering out like a fish.

Hisa gasped. Amazed. The pain had stopped and a baby! Out of her and into the world. "Thank you, God," she whispered. She started laughing. Weakly, but laughter all the same.

The flat sound rang in the silence.

Hisa stared at the medical staff huddled between her splayed knees. The baby –

Silent.

"No –"

A gurgle. Sound of suction. Squawk. A thin nasal wail.

The baby was alive.

Hisa sighed. Something maternal crept, bloomed in her heart and spread through her chest. "I want to see the baby," she said hoarsely. Proudly. She finally noticed a mirror set up so she could see her privates. She watched as an enormous blood clot slithered out from between her legs. It felt almost erotic.

"There's the placenta," someone said. It was slid into a silver dish. It looked like the cow livers sold in the markets.

Bobby started crying. Hisa smiled bravely. He must be so moved. So very happy, she thought. She raised her chin, bestowing a loving gaze toward him. I am a mother, she thought proudly.

Bobby turned away.

Her heart lurched. Gasped. She clutched her left breast.

"What's wrong!" Dear God, she hadn't checked for any defects. She was only thirty-one. She hadn't been advised to get an amniocentesis and she hadn't given it a second thought. But maybe it was Bobby. He was forty-three. Maybe his sperm was defective. And now it was too late. Oh, Lord, Hisa prayed, Lord let it be something minor. She just couldn't bear it if the child was severely handicapped.

"Let me see my baby," Hisa said loudly.

"It's a girl," the doctor said. She lowered her mask and smiled briskly. "She has to be weighed and measured and then you can see her. She's healthy and strong. You needn't worry."

"Baw-beeeeee," Hisa wailed.

Bobby dragged the back of his paw across his dripping nose. Rubbed the tears from his face with one shoulder, then the other. He pasted a smile on his face. "Baby," he said brightly. "What are we going to name her, hmmm? Something really pretty."

Hisa grabbed the sleeve of his yukata and yanked him closer. She clutched the tattered blue threads of his collar and held his face to hers. "What's wrong with it?" she whispered hoarsely. "Is its head misshapen? Does it – ?" Hisa gulped. "Does it have really slanted eyes?"

Bobby stared at her, perplexed. Glanced at the corners of Hisa's eyes.

"No!" Hisa hissed. "Not slanted like mine!"

Bobby's gaze darted over Hisa's features, looking for clues.

"The other kind of slanted," Hisa gritted. "The retarded kind!"

"Mrs Santos," the doctor said crisply. "There is nothing at this time which might suggest your baby is mentally or physically impaired. There is only a very minor superficial abnormality that can be rectified with a small surgical procedure."

All that Hisa retained was "abnormality." Abnormality tolled in her head like a death knell.

Hisa fell back on to the birthing table. "Oh, God," she whispered. Fat tears rolled down her cheeks. She covered her face with both hands. Hisa started sobbing.

"Shhhh," Bobby tried. "Sweetheart. It's nothing, really. I was just a little surprised. But like the doctor says, it's nothing that can't be fixed with a little surgery."

There was the sound of muffled raised voices. Banging doors and a waft of perfume ballooned in the room as someone entered on loud heels. As loud as a pony.

"Hisa!" a woman bellowed. "I'm here! Hisa!"

"Mama," Hisa whimpered.

Bobby was wrenched from his place and Junko's eyes, ringed completely in black kohl, gazed down at her daughter with a fierce adoration. The cloying sweet scent of *Poison* saturated the air. "Hisa-chan," she kissed her daughter's matted forehead. "They didn't want to let me in. I'm sorry I'm so late. Are you still in pain?"

"Mama, there's something w-wrong with the baby," Hisa blubbered.

Junko's more subtle emotions, masked with eye-liner and sky-blue shadow, were indistinguishable. But her expressive lips, a brilliant shade of orange-red, turned downward, two long creases etching from the corners to her jaw. She looked like a ventriloquist's doll. Her mouth flapped open, then shut. Nothing came out.

"Mama, what –"

Two large female nurses gently but firmly gripped Junko's upper arms.

"Let me go," she sprayed. "This is my daughter. I gave birth to her! What do you know about what she needs! I know her like I know my own body. Let me *go*! Hisa! Hisa!"

Junko's voice muffled as the door swung shut.

Bobby stepped back to his place beside Hisa. He smiled wanly. Hisa turned away. "I want to see my baby," she said numbly.

The doctor, smiling, brought the newborn to Hisa. The baby had a stretchy white toque on her head and was wrapped in cloth. "Seven pounds, three ounces," the doctor said. "Her face was slightly bruised as she came through the birth canal. But she's fine."

Hisa awkwardly clutched the bundle of baby to her chest. Her eyes darted frantically over the infant's face. Her complexion a mottled reddish purple, the baby's flat nose was covered with white-heads. It was hard to discern the true shape of her eyes. They were squinting tightly against the bright lights. Hisa didn't know what to feel. She's very ugly, she thought. But maybe she's not retarded. Hisa glanced around anxiously, then tugged the toque off the baby's head so that she could see the shape of the skull. The infant had thin, dark brown hair. No betraying lumps. Then she noticed. A fluttering on the baby's head. As large as a circle made by thumb and forefinger. The circle of skin was beating up and down. The baby had a hole in her head. . . .

"Ohmygod," Hisa gasped. "Her head!" Hisa's heart. It clenched, spasmodic. She couldn't breathe.

The doctor peered. "There's nothing wrong with this child's head," she said impatiently.

"That! The skin, there," Hisa pointed with her chin, both hands clutching the baby. "It's moving!"

"My dear," the doctor smiled. "That's the fontanelle. It's perfectly normal, though this fontanelle is a little bigger than usual. The bones of the skull don't completely fuse until up to eighteen months. But there's no cause for alarm. I would have thought you learned about this in your prenatal class."

Hisa sagged. Exhausted. "Then where's the abnormality?" she asked dully.

The doctor started to unbundle the infant. "It's very superficial," she said briskly. "Your daughter was born with a caudal appendage." The doctor expertly lifted the purplish squirming infant and held her face down in her capable hands. The baby feebly moved her legs.

Right where the crack of her buttocks began was a tail.

It was covered in skin and tapered at the tip.

It was about eight centimetres long.

Hisa stared. What moisture left in her mouth withered: a bitter dust on her tongue. Her heart boomed inside her ears.

The doctor flipped the baby right side up and rebundled her in the hospital cloth. "It looks like a tail, but it's not. A caudal appendage is mostly skin and either fatty substance or gristle-like material. It's not a true tail. It's more like a skin abnormality. Like a wen, if you will."

"Kobutori Jī-san," Hisa giggled. "Like the Japanese folk tale. 'The Old Man and His Wen.'"

"Precisely." The doctor handed the baby back to Hisa's reluctant arms. "You can try nursing if you like."

The baby's eyes were open. Glassy. Dark, with a bluish sheen. Hisa couldn't tell where the irises ended and the pupils began. The white pimples dotting her pug nose were unattractive. The baby's lips started working. Pinching, puckering, like she was just learning movement.

"When can you cut it off?" Hisa asked dully. Exhausted.

Bobby smiled wanly. Patted the baby's head with the back of his fingers.

The doctor's smile slipped into a quick frown. "We'll have to check scheduling. We might be able to complete the procedure before you're discharged." The doctor murmured something to the nurse and left the room. Just as she was leaving, Dr Armstrong burst through, his pale blue eyes blinking in the light.

"Aren't you the fast one," he enthused. "So where's your commonplace miracle?"

Hisa started weeping again.

Hisa's privates ached. As if she had been pounded with a bat. The blinds were drawn so she had no way of knowing if it was day or night, but some reptilian part of her brain suggested pre-dawn. The night-light cast a dim orange glow inside the room. A gurgling squeak. Tiredly, Hisa turned toward the sound.

The baby's clear plastic bassinet was at the foot of her bed. Hisa had breastfed the infant three times already. She didn't take very much. Hisa wished it was kept in the nursery. They had given her a choice, but she hadn't wanted the nursing staff to think she was cold and heartless, an abnormal woman who didn't want her own baby.

The infant snuffled and squawked. Maybe it would fall back asleep if she left it alone, Hisa thought hopefully. She clutched the thin hospital blankets to her chin, as if warding off bedtime monsters.

The baby snuffled, snorted. "Hhhhngha, hhhhngha, hhhh-hhngha," she warmed up. And cracked into a long and nasal wail.

Hisa struggled to her side and carefully eased her body off the bed. She shuffled to the baby and stared at the infant's face.

They hadn't named her yet. The names they had chosen before she was born tasted like ashes inside of Hisa's mouth now. Her eyes burned dry. The Rat. It was the year of the Rat, wasn't it?

The baby feebly batted her tiny fists in the dim light. The toque skewed sideways, covering one tightly squeezed eye. The thin nasal wail pierced Hisa through to her core. When she clasped her heart she could feel the damp of her breast.

The Lord has a reason for all things, Hisa thought dully. Doesn't He?

A nurse stuck her head through the doorway. "Do you need a hand?" she asked.

Hisa stared at her silhouette. Shook her head and tried to smile.

"Would you like me to change the diaper?" the nurse said gently.

Hisa had thought she had cried all of her tears. But her lashes were suddenly wet and she batted them fiercely, the light from the hallway refracting.

"I should start practicing," Hisa said bravely. "Don't you think?"

"If it feels right," the nurse nodded. "Are you feeling okay? Do you want to book a visit with the counsellor? You might have the baby blues. A lot of new mothers get that, you know. There's nothing to be ashamed of."

Hisa stepped back. As if she had been slapped. "I feel fine," she said. Suddenly, she wished Bobby had stayed. But he had gone home to get some rest and Mama had to be told not to visit until the next day. Hisa took a new diaper from the shelf below the bassinet. The baby had managed to unbundle herself from the swaddling cloth. Her small feet punctuated each raspy cry with sharp little kicks. Her toes so long they looked out of place. Hisa tentatively picked at the small tab of adhesive that kept the diaper shut.

The nurse still stood in the doorway.

"Go away!" Hisa snapped. "There must be other people who are more sick than I am." She couldn't see the nurse's face. Her voice had sounded young.

"There's no need," the nurse said slowly, "to take that kind of tone. We're here to protect the welfare of you and your baby." The nurse stood there. A dark shadow. The light from the hallway revealing Hisa's face. The nurse stared for as long as she wanted, then turned away. The soft squeaks of her shoes receded.

Hisa's eyes darted about. What did the nurse think of her? Was that the same nurse as before or a new one? Why were they hanging around her? Hisa covered her mouth with her fingers, horrified. Did they think she'd do something to the baby? Hisa vigorously shook her head. No! She wasn't like that.

Was she?

Maybe the nursing station was awash with the news of the baby with a tail. Each new shift bringing in new spectators. Maybe they all wanted to see it. Like the poor Elephant Man. . . .

Meanwhile, the baby had cried herself well beyond nasal wails into a heart-piercing rasp.

"Oh, oh!" Hisa flustered. "Shhhh, babygirl. Shhhhhh." She clasped the infant to her chest and hobbled to the chair by the window. She had to shush her fast. Before another spy nurse came by. She opened the flap on her mint-green gown and awkwardly juggled one breast out of the bra. The baby, smelling the milk, rooted around for the source. Hisa crammed the nipple into the baby's open mouth like she'd been taught. It was a bad latch. The baby was sucking voraciously on the tip instead of firmly around the whole nipple. Hisa let her be. Bore the pain.

The baby was cushioned on the loose bag of her stomach. The infant's right hand rested on Hisa's full breast and with each suck, her tiny fingers squeezed against the skin. Her hand was so graceful. The nurse had cut the baby's fingernails because they were so long at birth.

Really, Hisa thought, she looks so normal like this.

The baby fed for about five minutes. Then she stopped. Her pucker of mouth still lipping Hisa's nipple, the baby had fallen asleep again.

Hisa gently rose and shuffled to the bassinet. She could just put her back without changing the diaper.

Good thoughts, her mother had said. Psychically linked. Hisa didn't believe in all that, but the Bible said love all of the creatures, great and small. Or was that from somewhere else? Hisa shook her head. Jesus had eaten with harlots and befriended lepers. This baby was of her own flesh and blood!

Hisa pulled her lips tight with determination. Quickly, before she could change her mind, she peeled the tabs off the diaper and dropped the front open.

152

A stump stuck from the baby's belly! The colour of dried blood. Hisa's stomach churned. When she realized it was the remains of the umbilical cord, she feebly laughed aloud.

The baby's labia were swollen, but normal. A gluey greenish poo was smeared in the diaper.

Where was the tail?

Hisa clasped the baby's small ankles in one hand and lifted slowly.

The baby's bottom, smeared in the dark sticky fecal matter, was a mess.

The tail. It had been positioned upward, along the baby's back, the base pressed tightly against its natural resting position.

"Oh," Hisa gasped. It looked terribly uncomfortable! She supposed the last person to change the diaper had done that so the tail – the caudal appendage – wouldn't be fouled by the feces. She knew people suggested that babies didn't really have nerve endings like adults or even children. That's why it was still okay for male babies to get the skin of their little penises ripped off with no anesthetic. But Hisa wasn't so sure. Surely, if she pinched the infant, she would wake up and start bawling.

Hisa wiped the dirty bum and remembered to swab the belly button stump with the alcohol and Q-tip. She did it as quickly as she could. Her hands icy. The baby squirmed in her half-sleep. Hisa didn't want her to wake up.

Hisa didn't put on the clean diaper.

She stared at the tail.

It didn't look very different from a thin finger. Finger, Hisa thought. Innocuous as a finger. If she looked at it long enough, would she lose this skin-crawling repulsion? Because she could admit it. To herself. The tail was horrible. A freak of nature that was wrong, wrong, wrong!

Hisa's hands shook. She loosed her hold on the baby's ankles. Breathed slowly, deeply, her exhalations breaking up into shudders.

"It's Bobby's fault," Hisa whispered. Bobby and his old sperm.

"My fault," a voice croaked.

She shrieked. Clasped the baby to her chest. The tail. She was touching the tail. . . . Warm. Firm. As thick as a pencil. Hisa's skin crawled.

Someone. In the doorway. A squat form and hair. Hair standing wild and uncombed like someone from a madhouse! Hisa backed slowly to the head of her bed. The nurse call button –

"Hisa-chan. I had to come back."

"Mama?" Hisa said incredulously. "Mama?"

"Can I come in?" she asked humbly.

"Of course. Shut the door. Turn on the light. There's no lock. Mama, what's wrong?" Hisa's lower lip started to wobble. She'd never seen her mama like this before. So – undone.

The sudden buzz of fluorescent lights glared hideously on Junko's face. Without make-up her mother was unrecognizable. Dark creases bagged her eyes and her eyelids were wrinkled like the skin of naked mole rats. Her pale lips were barely visible, an apparition of a mouth. She was lost in her own face. She must have brushed out her curls, but she hadn't restyled them. Her mama looked like she had just jumped out of bed. And that was unheard of.

"I had to tell you," Junko managed. She took two faltering steps toward her daughter. Then stopped. "You have to know."

Hisa shook her head. This news. She didn't want to hear it. Whatever it was that had ruined her mother, she didn't want the knowledge. "No, Mama," Hisa wobbled. "You said. Nice things. Nice thoughts. That's what you said, Mama. I can't bear anymore."

"You must!" Junko hissed. "You're a mother now! You must listen!"

Fat tears rolled down Hisa's face. The salt burned her dry skin. She wept without sound. Shoulders dropping, she closed her eyes and gasped, shuddered for air. She wiped her nose with a corner of the baby's swaddling cloth, then looked upon her mother's old face. "Tell me, then," Hisa said defeatedly.

Junko raised her head. The folds of skin beneath her chin quivered.

"You had a tail, too."

The room ballooned, a sudden vacuum. Captured. Then, every sound resonated as isolated overblown entities inside Hisa's mind. The fluorescent light buzzed with frenetic electrons. Granules of dust slid across the glass window, one tiny mote after the other. The furnace clicked with the change of temperature, the pipes expanding atom by atom. The baby's breathing split into air, heart, blood, hemoglobin. Hisa gasped. The world cracked. Then the shards slid back to create an entire picture once more.

Hisa turned her head, leaned slightly sideways, and retched dryly. Junko held out her arms for the baby and Hisa quickly dropped the child as her stomach convulsed once more. All she brought up was bitter fluid. Her throat burned and she spat into the bedpan. When she could turn back to her mother, Junko had finished fixing the diaper and was staring into the baby's sleeping face. Hisa couldn't read her mama's expression. Without the make-up, Junko was a stranger.

Hisa sucked in her breath.

Three miscarriages, her mother had always told her.

And Hisa the only survivor.

How could she know if her mother had told the truth? What if – what if her mother had borne living monsters and she had smothered them, one after the other. . . .

Hisa snatched her baby out of her mother's arms. "Why are you telling me now?"

Junko blinked watery eyes. "So you don't go through the same things I did." She turned away.

Hisa tried to gulp. Her tongue stuck to the roof of her mouth, clacked horribly. "What things," she asked hoarsely. "What did you do to them?"

Junko raised her trembling fingers. Toward her only daughter. Hisa stepped backward with her child, raising her shoulder slightly so that the infant was out of her mother's reach. Junko's wretched face fell open. "Noooo," she wailed. "No!"

"What's going on?" Two nurses marched through the door, quickly assessing the situation. "Mrs Santos needs her rest right now. Please leave immediately and do not return until proper visiting hours. If you cannot follow regulations we will have to call security." The nurses ushered Junko out of the room as efficiently as prison guards.

Junko craned her neck over her shoulder. "Hisa-chan! Don't make the same mistake I did!"

By the time the nurses came back, Hisa had placed the sleeping infant in the bassinet and now lay in her narrow hospital bed, the thin blankets pulled over her head.

"Are you okay?" A warm hand cupped her shoulder. Hisa flinched and the hand dropped away. Hisa shook her head.

"Would you like us to take the baby to the nursery?"

"Please," Hisa's voice cracked.

Nurses murmuring, the slow squeaky wheels of the bassinet rattled to the door.

"Wait," Hisa jolted upright.

The nurses stopped.

"Don't let *her* near the baby," she said fiercely.

"Someone will stay with your child," a nurse soothed. "You sleep, now. You need your rest."

156

Hisa lay back down. An icy weight settled next to her heart. Dawn tried to breach her room, but Hisa turned away from the window and closed her eyes. She was waiting. Waiting for comfort from the Holy Spirit or Jesus Christ. But all she heard was her heart booming inside her eardrums. "God forgive you," she whispered hoarsely.

Bobby arrived with a huge vase of white lilies, her overnight bag, a mothering magazine, and her favourite pair of shoes. The perfume of the sweet cloying flowers filled the room. Hisa's stomach rolled over itself, the half bowl of porridge she had managed to eat moiling toward gag reflex.

"Sweetie pie," Bobby bent to drop a kiss in Hisa's matted hair. "Where's our beautiful daughter?"

"Lilies are for dead people," Hisa blurted, then burst into tears.

Bobby's first-time-father's face slipped askew. His lower lip drooped, but he valiantly erased his pout and managed to fix a smile in place as he set the flowers out of sight on the bathroom counter. He bustled to his sobbing wife and curled his hot arm around her shaking shoulders, nudging her with his belly. Hisa instinctively moved over though she could feel the small stitches keeping her vagina together tearing as she dragged her buttocks sideways across the mattress.

Bobby's thick arm under her neck, Hisa's head was thrust out at an awkward angle. The smells particular to Bobby pooled thickly around her face.

"Shhhhhhh," Bobby whispered into her ear as he spooned into his wife's sorrow. Hot tears burned as they slid sideways across her face.

"I heard from the psychologist that you've been crying all night," Bobby soothed.

Hisa, sobbing, bobbed her head.

"That Mama came to see you and she upset you even more."

Hisa's sobs shook her as Bobby's body jostled against her back-side, the hot cup of his manhood. He pressed into the cushions of her buttocks, his sweet and sour breath moistening the air. Hisa could feel Bobby's penis against the crack of her buttocks. Growing hard, bony, like a thick tail. . . .

She shrieked. Flailed her arms, flutter-kicked her feet. Bobby squawked as he fell backwards out of the narrow bed.

He didn't rise.

Hisa fearfully peered over the edge.

Bobby's eyes were squeezed shut. His chest moved rapidly with his breath.

"Bobby," Hisa whispered hoarsely. "Bobby. Are you okay?"

"Phsssssst," he managed. A hiss between pursed lips.

"Did you hurt something, Bobby? Do you want me to call for the nurse?"

"Sss, sssssst."

"Well," Hisa stared dubiously, "if you're sure." The ripped stitches in her perineum jabbed needles of pain. Hisa slowly rolled over and stared blearily at the white square panels on the ceiling. She didn't know why they did that. Designing the slabs to look like they'd been bored through by termites. There must be something wrong with her.

A plat, plat, plat of sound. Hisa turned her head. Bobby was crawling toward the chair. He clung to the armrests and pulled him-self upright, a small muscle jumping in his cheek. He hissed like a deflating tire as he sat down on the seat.

Bobby's emotionless demeanor was worthy of a samurai. Hisa tried a smile.

"I believe," Bobby said carefully, "I'll go home for the rest of the day and return in the evening."

Hisa bit her lip. "Are you angry with me?" she asked tearfully.

"Of course not," Bobby said.

"You're angry with me."

"Darling," Bobby rose stiffly from the chair and shuffled to her side. He started bending, then grimaced. Slowly, slowly stood ram-rod straight again. "You mean everything to me. I'm a lesser man without you. You complete me." He clasped her cold fingers with his bear-like paw and raised them to his lips. He kissed the back of her hand. "I'll be back in the evening."

"I love you?" Hisa whispered.

"I love you, too." Bobby reassured. "Don't you worry about the baby, sweetheart. I've signed the papers. They're doing the procedure tomorrow. When we go home together we'll be like any other family. And no one need ever know."

"No one ever need know," Hisa murmured. The warm water lapped against the soggy sack of her belly. She hadn't wanted to take a sitz bath. She was afraid that her privates would sting and burn, like the flayed rabbit in the folk tale who was tricked into smearing hot peppers into its skin. But the salty warm water felt good and the pain in her perineum eased. Who would have thought?

"No one ever need know," she sing-songed. Her voice echoed against the tiles of the private bathroom. "No one ever need know."

Just like her. She hadn't known and she was fine.

A child like everyone else.

Raised by a single mother. Birthdays celebrated. A graduation trip to Venice paid for by her father. A modest career as a floral de-signer with a small but loyal client-base.

How long had her tail been?

Hisa blinked rapidly. Biting her lip she slowly, cautiously, slid her hand beneath her body. Stared anxiously at the closed door. What if someone came in? Her flesh pimpling with fear and revulsion, foreign, her own foreign body, she palmed down her right buttock.

"Uhunnn," Hisa gulped, half a sob, half a plea.

She probed the juncture of her buttocks with her forefinger.

. . .

Nothing. Nothing.

She started giggling. A gulping laugh-cry.

Oh.

There.

There was . . . a ridge of skin.

A . . . bump.

She jerked her hand away, panting hard as blood surged in her ears, her brain. A high-pitched whine filled her head and she squeezed her eyes to stop. The ceiling spun even without sight.

Lord Jesus. Mercy upon me. Count your blessings. Salvation of angels. The meek and the mild. Love the lepers. Blessed are the deformed. The kindness of hunchbacks. Mark of the beast –

"Give it back!" she rasped. Mama! Mama who had to tell her now! She'd been forced to eat of the fruit when she would rather have lived on in the Garden! "Give the Garden back to me!"

The bath water was cold. All she could do was step out, shivering, and wipe herself dry.

Hisa crawled naked into the narrow hospital bed. Stared upward at the termite-patterned ceiling.

She had been an amputee her whole life, without knowing it.

What did that make her?

She could never tell Bobby. Ever! Bobby would never understand. Bobby liked Japanese girls. Yukatas and hot springs. Bobby didn't even like bananas.

Hisa thought back as far as she could remember. Where family photos blurred with experienced events. Hadn't she always felt that something had been missing? She used to think she was missing siblings. The particular loneliness of being an only child. Then she met Bobby and she thought she'd found that missing thing.

How many amputated tailless people were out there. . . ?

"Lord, Lord, Lord, Lord," Hisa crooned.

Babygirl, too.

No one ever need know.

"What does it matter?" Hisa hissed. "I'm still the same as I was yesterday. The day before. Nothing I've done changes. I'm still me!"

"No, you're not."

"I am!"

"You cannot think of yourself in the same way."

"The world, my experiences haven't changed!"

"Haven't your feelings changed?"

"I'm just surprised. Who wouldn't be?"

"You must feel confused. Betrayed. Loss."

"I'm still me. . . ."

"Do you think you'd be the same person if your tail hadn't been removed?"

"What are you saying! No one could live in this world with a tail! You'd have to join a circus! A freak show! It's not really a tail. It's a skin growth. Fatty gristle. The doctor said. Leave me alone." Hisa yanked the thin blanket over her head.

"Don't lie to yourself. It won't help anything."

"Go away!" Hisa shrieked.

"Mrs Santos, do you need anything?" a cheerful voice called from the doorway.

Hisa jerked the blanket off her head and patted her frowsy hair, smiling, smiling. "I must have been having a nightmare," she laughed feebly. "Did I say anything?"

The nurse wheeled the squeaky bassinet into the room. "You were shouting. I'm going to check your temperature. Baby just woke up for a feeding." The nurse stuck the gauge into Hisa's ear. "Normal," she chirped. And deftly deposited the infant into Hisa's arms. The nurse matter-of-factly squidged, squidged down the hallway. Hisa awkwardly inched herself into a sitting position, the baby jostling from side to side, squirming, almost spasmodic.

She stared into the infant's glassy eyes. Maybe a student nurse would mix her up with someone else's baby and she could take home a normal one.

Hisa laid the infant down on her outstretched legs. She yanked the bundled cloth, jerking the fold across and down, revealing the baby's bare legs, her long slender feet. The infant screwed up her face, the ugly red skin beginning to turn purple. "Hhhhngha, hhhhngha, hhhhhngha," she warmed up. Hisa tugged the strings holding the baby smock together and yanked them open. The adhesive tabs of the diaper ripped. Hisa flipped the baby over. Grabbed the infant beneath her armpits and dangled the deformity in front of her face.

The baby threw out her arms, her body rigid, in a Moro's reflex.

The caudal appendage. The skin abnormality.

It looked longer in the daylight. Pink. Like a rat. Hisa stared and stared. Her mouth dry. Open.

The baby screamed, legs kicking, her head lolling to one side.

And the caudal appendage.

It jerked.

Hisa gaped. No! She must have jostled the thing. The doctor said it was no more than extra skin. Just a growth. No nerve endings. No connecting bones. . . .

The slender pink length. Twitched. Fitfully. An uncontrolled movement. Like the flailing of her baby arms and legs. Then it slid. Across Hisa's skin, a rush of goose flesh rippling up her arm, the nape of her neck. Warm, warmer than her body temperature, the skin smooth and covered in fine hairs . . . the tail twined tightly around Hisa's wrist in a reflex of survival. Gripped closely, solid, as if she'd never let go.

Hisa almost dropped her.

The rasping cries of the baby finally reached Hisa's brain. She clamped the infant to her naked chest, cramming her nipple into the baby's distraught mouth. Latching, she started sucking deeply, snorting for air through her nostrils.

The tail still circled Hisa's wrist. The baby gazed up at her face.

Hisa could only gape.

She knew the baby couldn't really see. That the baby saw mostly shapes of dark and light, colour and movement. But the baby could taste, and smell her too. Hear. Hadn't Hisa sung songs to her when she was still in her uterus? The vibrations, the pitch. Didn't some people say they remembered being inside the womb?

"Nemureyo iko-you," Hisa whispered her favourite lullaby.

The baby stared at her. Black eyes dark with secrets. The tail's grip tightened ever so slightly.

"Niwa, yama kiba mou," Hisa sang. Her voice trembled, but something was expanding inside her chest, suffusing her with warmth.

"When the birds and the sheep
All should fall asleep
The moon, through the window
Shines its silver light
Flowing through this night
Sleep good child, sleep."

The baby, curved around her breast, breathed quickly, deeply. Her eyelids closed. Her mouth was still puckered around Hisa's nipple. A pale pink bracelet around Hisa's wrist. She held the baby close to her heart, rocked slowly back and forth.

"What happened to my tail?" Hisa whispered into the telephone.

"Oh!" Mama gasped. "Hisa-chan. I love you so much. You have no idea –"

"Yes, Mama. I know. What happened to my tail?" she hissed.

"It was a hard thing, Hisa-chan. It was a hard labour. I'd lost three babies before you. Three! It breaks a mother's heart. All of them in the third trimester. They were almost ready. Just about ready. But something would happen. They came out too soon. And you were my last chance! They said I couldn't try any more."

"The others. Did they have tails, too?"

Her Mama gulped hard, like she was swallowing shards of glass.

"Yes. They all had tails." Hisa could hear the sadness in her mother's voice. "But yours was the longest!" Mama added quickly.

"Did my tail . . . move? It wasn't a skin growth, was it?"

"Hisa-chan. I was weak. I was forty-two when I had you. I was confused. You lived. But you had a tail, like the others. Your father, my husband, " Mama spat. "He left that night."

Hisa's cheeks burned.

"That night. I felt your tail twitching beneath the wet cloth diaper. I – I screamed. They came and took you away. Sedated me. When I woke up the next afternoon your tail was gone."

A searing heat crackled inside Hisa's chest. Her breath was short and the clamour of bells resounded inside her head.

"Hisa-chan. I'm so sorry. I didn't protect you. Please forgive your mama," Mama sobbed.

Hisa heard an audible *click* inside her ears. Like a jackknife being opened. Then everything was clear.

"I need your help now," Hisa stated.

"Yes, yes, anything!"

Hisa whispered instructions as her mother scratched out the details on a piece of paper.

And despite the clarity in her head, Hisa was still frightened. Where would they go? What would they do? What did she know about being abnormal, living as abnormals? She had no skills or experience in that realm. And how would she begin to find the others like her and her baby?

"Oh!" Hisa gasped. Of course! *They* would help her. Oh, it wasn't the same thing, exactly, but they would have an inkling of what she was going through. What was their number? Biting her lip she tried to wipe the anxiety away and just let her fingers tap out the buttons as if she was being guided by the Holy Spirit.

The phone rang seven times.

"Hello!" a voice snapped.

"Hello?" Hisa meekly asked. "Is – is this Maggie and Julia's residence?" She didn't even know their last name. Names.

"Who is this? Do you know what time it is?"

"I'm so sorry," Hisa gushed. Eyes frantically looking for a clock. Her watch. "It's Hisa. I'm calling from the hospital."

"Hisa? I don't know any Hisa."

"Oh!" Hisa gasped. She hadn't thought of that. And she'd been so nice to them during the prenatal classes! "Please. We were in the same baby classes. At the community centre," she added humbly.

"Ohhhh," Julia said. "I'm sorry," her voice sounding sweeter. "It must be the lack of sleep. We had our baby last week, you know."

"Congratulations," Hisa managed.

"What about you?" Julia asked, warming slightly. "Did you have your baby, too?"

"I – I did," Hisa gulped. Clarity clouding with sudden sadness. "A girl. I have a baby girl."

"Oh," Julia sounded like she was smiling. "That's lovely."

"I have a favour to ask!" Hisa blurted.

"What do you mean?" Caution creeping into Julia's voice.

"My baby isn't normal! She – shehasatail!"

"Oh," Julia murmured.

"They want to cut it off!" Hisa almost shrieked. Caught herself. "I don't know if they should. What if she's meant to have it?" she whispered hoarsely.

"Hisa, maybe this is something to discuss with your doctor and the baby's father," Julia said gently.

"I can't! Bobby's signed the papers already. They'll never let her keep it. They'll say it's a deformity and she'd never be treated like a normal child if she had a tail. You would know what that's like."

"What?" Julia's voice tight.

"What it's like not to be normal," Hisa explained eagerly. "That's why I called. Because you're the only people I know who might help us. . . ."

"You have some nerve! Jesus Christ!"

Hisa flinched.

"You call us in the middle of the night because in your stupid, sheltered, middle-class, heterosexual mind you think we're 'not normal' and that we'll help you because we can identify with your tailed freak baby?" Julia shouted.

"Oh!" Hisa gasped. She started weeping. "Oh, oh."

"Hello!" A low harsh voice rasped.

Hisa shook her head. She had been so mistaken.

"Stop your bawling," Maggie said hoarsely.

"I'm sorry," Hisa gulped. "I'm sorry to bother you."

"Shut up," Maggie said. "Just write down our address."

Hisa could hear Julia's raised voice in the background.

"Thank you!" Hisa gushed. "Maggie. Thank you so much."

"Shut up," Maggie sighed. "I'm not making any promises. You can come over for now, that's all."

"Is it okay if my mother meets us there?" Hisa asked humbly.

"Christ! Yeah. Okay, your mother can come, too. Jesus."

"Maggie! I'm this close to –" Hisa could hear Julia's tinny voice in the background.

"Yeah, what if Karlyn hadn't bailed you out when you were sixteen?" Maggie snapped. "Where'd do you think you'd be now?"

"Don't mind Julia," Maggie rasped. "I'll talk to her. Her heart's in the right place."

"Maggie. I don't know what to say," Hisa began.

"Save it. What did you name your baby?"

"I haven't chosen one yet," Hisa said guiltily.

"We have a great name book," Maggie said. "Come on over. I'll put on a pot of mint tea."

Hisa hung up the phone, her heart buoyed with a small measure of hope. Then she slumped. She stared at the palms of her hands. How could everything change so quickly? Just yesterday or the day before she'd been such an innocent. Hisa shook her head. She could have lived her whole life an innocent, and been perfectly happy for all she knew. And after all, what was a woman to do? What was a mother to do?

She changed into day clothes and packed her overnight bag with the diapers and bundling cloths that were stored below the bassinet. Luckily she had her purse already. She would have enough money to finance travel. And Mama had her savings, too. It would be enough to see them to warmer climes. Like that childhood game. When someone or something was hidden. And you had to guess where. A friend would tell you if you were getting closer. "Warmer, warmer, warmer," Hisa murmured.

She would sneak into several other bedrooms and press their

nurse call buttons so that no one would witness her departure. She supposed there were security cameras. Hisa wondered if she ought to soap the lenses. But there was no point. Once she'd left, watching her image on video wasn't going to tell them where she was. She wondered if she should leave Bobby a note. But, really, there was nothing she could say that would explain. And in time, he would forget all about her. Be secretly relieved that he wouldn't have to face his daughter every day. Their disappearance wouldn't be remarkable. They would just be another few women, lost.

She darted out and shuffled down the hallway. Ducked into one room. A few doors down. Then another. She darted back to her room. The stitches in her perineum stabbed slivers of pain. Hisa bundled her baby with two more layers of cloth. Pressed her lips to her forehead, the sweet smell of milk filling her nostrils. Hisa clasped the overnight bag and purse with one elbow, then carefully lifted her baby into her arms. "Nenne," she murmured. "Nenne."

She heard the squidge squidge squidge of shoes going past her door. The soft murmur of voices.

Heart pounding, Hisa held her baby snug. She stepped through the doorway and walked down the long, clean hallway. The bite of pine cleanser and ammonia. The sound of babies squawking behind closed doors.

She could feel something behind her.

Hisa's heart clenched.

She did not look over her shoulder.

A weight. A balance. A graceful length that slid through air, weaving a subtle pattern.

Hisa smiled.

All Possible Moments

Sunlight drapes a thin orange fabric and the breeze describes the movement. The clothes ebb and flow. I watch you breathing the hot summer air. The library was cool after the mid-day pavement, cars exhausting all possibilities of a still moment. That afternoon. The subject of love and the object of love were filed together. The yellow index cards creased and stained with thousands of hands before me. Tens of thousands. Hundreds of thousands, how could I know? I caught my breath. A woman looked up from her cool, smooth table and our eyes met for a moment. Threads of saffron, gold, and blood oranges. The fabric breathes with your breath. The play of light through silky fibres. Your skin. The whirring hum of cold air circulated through the glass room. Frowning, sweating patrons stumbled through the automatic doors, a moment of loss and confusion when the summer heat turned into cool reflection. Oblique anticipation. A shiver of breath across sticky foreheads, half-circles of sweat cupping their armpits. Their cells died. Every day. Water lifting off skin, a salty residue. They came for books on hold, special collections, translations of molecules. Out of the volume of heat into a container of quiet. "Of Love" the index card read. Subject/Object. The index cards filled five-and-one-third long, wooden drawers. Moth. Mother. Mouth. "Mouth," I mouthed. Did they mean lips? Lost Love. Lover's Leap. Love's Lie. The heart leapt. Then pattered back to normalcy. Your skin darker than cedar. The sun's gold catches in the fine hairs of your arms. The dappled play of light ripples like water. Fresh. A book lying face-down, waiting to be read. A book I will read. Breathe. A whisk of sound, soft soles on cold marble floors. The cart creaked with books, hard soft covers beading with condensation. The librarian's mouth pinched disapproval. A towel draped over one shoulder. "Air conditioning," she muttered. And strode toward a small door marked Private. Water droplets marked her passage. I licked the beading above my upper lip. Closed my eyes. A cool trickle of air flickered across my skin, my back shuddering spine. You roll over, your leg sliding from beneath the thin cotton sheet. The muscle curves, dimples behind your knee, a pocket of summer cupping heat. I purse my lips and blow gently. The thin orange curtain waxing and waning with my breath. Breathing. Dizzy, my hand dropped on open drawer. The heavy wood collided with the cold floor, the sharp sound ringing down long hallways, the high ceilings, patrons jerked from narratives of first love, lost loves, longing. Startling beyond subject and object. The index cards fluttered like leaves, flower petals. Sara, sara, sara, sara. Para, para, para, para. That afternoon. Picking up the index cards of love the insides of my hands were saturated with something oily. I was repulsed before I felt desire. It seeped into my skin. The perfume held within my cells. By the time the librarian and her assistant returned, annoyed and brisk, I was drunk on the smell. It filled the room, condensation running down the glass of tall windows. People rose from their chairs, left open books on cold tables, and waded dreamily back into the summer heat. The thin orange curtain cannot keep it out. But the breeze prevails, describing all possible movements. The waxing and waning of your breath. Breathing. You smile in your sleep as I wait your waking. A book face down on the floor beside the bed. Oblique anticipation.

Your eyes open.

Acknowledgments

Thank you to all who have made this book possible. My family, friends, communities surround me, and my writing life and living life spill messily and joyfully into all arenas. Thank you to Koji and Sae for keeping me real and sharing with me the magic of your lives. My gratitude and love to my family, near and far. Tamotsu, Kyoko, Naoe, Naomi, Nozomi, Chris, and Craig, your support is every writer's dream come true. Tiger, thank you for teaching me early to delight in the absurdities of life. Your ganbare attitude, generosity, and big laughter during hard times I truly respect. And thank you, Ayumi (my sissssterrr), for always letting me know you believe in my writing.

I cannot express my gratitude to dear friends, Rita and Tamai, who've graciously answered my middle-of-the-night-pleas-for-feedback-before-the-deadline calls. Bless your generous hearts.

Ashok, could anyone else have a sweeter, kinder, separated-at-birth-twin brother than you? I think not. (Plus, you make a damn fine martini. . . .)

Thank you, dear friends, whose love, humour and support keep me smiling in spite of the (global) madness. Especially Rita, for tonkatsu sleep-overs and your love of sweet mackerel, Susanda, for your gift of listening and sharing your laughter, and Eva, for the fine

lunches, cutting to the core of the matter, and your poetic heart. Big hugs to Ivana, Larissa, Ritz, and Aruna, my life would be dreary without you.

Roy, you're a great (and funny) travel buddy! Thank you for supporting my work.

Rita, Chieko, Margarida, thank you so much for all your help with child-care. Writers who are mothers could never make it unless they have people like you in their lives.

Editors who have helped me through earlier drafts of these stories are gratefully acknowledged. Aritha van Herk, Nalo Hopkinson, Emily Pohl-Weary, Alana Wilcox, Rosemary Nixon and the fiction editors at *Ms*, thank you for your keen eyes, astute observations. I am also thankful to Leslie Ellestad for medical feedback. Errors of facts (or outright weirdnesses) are my own.

A few of these stories go back many years. I would like to acknowledge my classmates in the fiction courses at the University of Calgary and my wonderful teachers there, Aritha van Herk and Fred Wah.

The fabulous folks at Arsenal Pulp Press: my thanks to Blaine, Brian, Kiran, Trish, and Robert. I'm so happy to have a book with you.

The title story was influenced, in part, by Wendy Pearson's excellent paper, "Sex/uality and the Hermaphrodite in Science Fiction, or, The Revenge of Herculine Barbin" published in *Edging into the Future: Science Fiction and Contemporary Cultural Transformation*, University of Pennsylvania Press, 2002. The quote on "hopeful monsters" is based on a 1977 article by Stephen Jay Gould entitled "The Return of Hopeful Monsters" published in *Natural History 86* (June/July): 22–30. The quotes on breastfeeding in "Tales from the Breast" were found in *Your Child's First Journey* by Brinkley, Goldberg, and Kukar, 1988, 2nd edition. The cover image of this book is a dental x-ray taken by Barb Sindell. Thanks to Sandra Semchuk who suggested the image be used for the cover.

The follwing stories were previously published in slightly different versions: "Night" in *West Coast Line*, Spring 1993 and subsequently anthologized in *Making a Difference: Canadian Multicultural Literature*, 1996. "Tilting" in *Boundless Alberta*, Aritha van Herk (ed), Newest Press, 1993. "Tales from the Breast" first published as "Are You A Suitable Candidate to Breastfeed Your Baby?" in *absinthe*, Winter 1995 and subsequently published in *Ms* and anthologized in *Witpunk*, Claude Lalumière and Marty Halpern (eds), 2003. "Stinky Girl" in *Due West*, Aritha van Herk (ed), 1996, and *Girls Who Bite Back*, Emily Pohl-Weary (ed), 2004. "Osmosis" in *Millennium Messages*, Kenda D. Gee and Wei Wong (eds), 1998. "Drift" in *Ms*, Volume ix, No. 3, April/May 1999. "Home Stay" in *WestCoastLine*, No. 29, 33/2, Fall 1999 and subsequently anthologized in *And Other Stories*, George Bowering (ed), 2001. "From Across a River" in *This Magazine*, Winter 2001. "All Possible Moments" in *Windsor Review*, 2004.

I would like to gratefully acknowledge the generous support of The Alberta Foundation for the Arts, the Canada Council for the Arts, and especially the 2003–04 writer-in-residency at the Emily Carr Institute of Art and Design in conjunction with the University of Northern British Columbia and Powell Street Festival.

photo: Sita Kumar

HIROMI GOTO is the author of the novels *The Kappa Child*, winner of the James Tiptree, Jr Award, and *Chorus of Mushrooms*, winner of the Commonwealth Writers Prize for First Book (Canada-Caribbean) and co-winner of the Canada-Japan Book Award, and the children's book *The Water of Possibility*, a selection of the Canadian Children's Book Centre. She lives in Burnaby, B.C.